Killer's Bounty

Forced to leave a wagon train, ex-gunfighter Saul Beck and his wife Mary seek refuge in a town called Calico Junction. But their journey leads them through Indian country and they fall prey to the Apache. Fortunately, they are rescued by the territory's biggest ranch owner, John Calico. From the outset, however, Saul clashes with John Calico's son, Tod, and trouble seems inevitable.

Then, when Saul uncovers a murder, he triggers off a chain of events that leads him to a face from the past who is looking for revenge. As his past rushes to catch up with him, it looks as if he must, once again, buckle on his gun before he can finally lay it to rest.

Killer's Bounty

Jack Holt

A Black Horse Western

ROBERT HALE · LONDON

© James O'Brien 2004
First published in Great Britain 2004

ISBN 0 7090 7514 6

Robert Hale Limited
Clerkenwell House
Clerkenwell Green
London EC1R 0HT

Typeset by
Derek Doyle & Associates, Liverpool.
Printed and bound in Great Britain by
Antony Rowe Limited, Wiltshire

CHAPTER ONE

'Damn it, Beck, can't you keep that wagon on a straight run?' Dan Bassett, the wagon master escorting the wagon train of which Saul Beck and his wife were a part, glared angrily at Beck. 'You're holding up the train. We're losing time in dangerous country, man. Your shenanigans will get us all killed.'

'That's a fact,' a man on a nearby wagon growled. 'Don't ya know that this is 'Pache country, Beck.'

'Keep your voice down, Sullivan!' The wagon master rebuked the man. 'Most folk in this train don't know that this is Apache country. But if you keep spouting, they soon will.'

'I'm doing the best I can, Bassett,' Beck growled, struggling to control the wagon's erratic progress.

'That rear left-side wheel ain't none too good,' Sullivan unnecessarily reminded Beck. 'Wobblin' like a Saturday-night drunk.'

'I didn't hear anyone ask you for your opinion, Sullivan,' Beck barked, his grey eyes blazing.

Bassett asked: 'Didn't you bust a wheel aways back, Beck?'

'Sure did,' Sullivan said.

Beck swept back a dark fringe of hair from his forehead. 'I can speak for myself, Sullivan.'

'Yeah, I remember,' Bassett said, frowning with displeasure. He rested on his saddle horn. 'That means that you haven't got a spare.'

Saul Beck said confidently: 'Won't need one.'

'What if that other wheel busts?' Sullivan's question was directed at Bassett.

'There's no way we can sit pretty, Beck,' the wagon master informed Saul. 'We've got to keep moving.'

'You can't just abandon us, Mr Bassett,' Mary Beck pleaded, her sea-blue eyes fearfully scanning the barren desert country. 'Mr Sullivan mentioned Apaches.'

'Easy, Mary.' Beck counselled his wife. He told Bassett: 'That wheel's solid.'

His bluff cut no ice with Dan Bassett.

'Hah! I figure that pretty soon that wheel will bust open like an overripe melon,' Sullivan opined. 'Best if you cut that wagon out right now, Bassett.'

'Saul,' Mary Beck pleaded, 'what about the baby?'

'Baby?' Bassett yelped. He turned furious eyes

6

on Beck. 'You knew the rules before you joined this train, mister. And one of them stated quite clearly that pregnant women were not welcome.'

'Mary wasn't sure when we started out,' Beck said in his defence. 'We were a week out when she was, and then there was no turning back.'

Bassett shook his head. 'Well, there sure as hell ain't no turning back now.'

Beck said: 'Maybe someone else has a spare we could buy.'

The wagon master snorted. 'Are you serious? Some of these wagons have two spares, but no one's going to sell you one, just in case they'll find themselves in the same predicament as you are in now, Beck.'

His angry eyes looked over Beck's ramshackle wagon. He shook his head.

'I never should have let you join this train. Not with a rig that's likely to fall 'part any second. There's a town, 'bout ten miles due east of here. A burg called Calico Junction. Named after John Calico, the owner of the biggest spread in these parts. I reckon you should cut out and head for there, Beck.'

'Alone?' Saul Beck asked.

'No other way. In the main these are all family men with responsibilities, Beck. Don't hold out much hope that one of them will leave his family to detour to Calico Junction with you folk. And I wouldn't ask anyone to do so.'

'I guess that's asking a lot, sure enough,' Beck agreed.

'We've got a couple of single men. But . . .' Bassett shrugged to indicate the hopelessness of Saul Beck's plight.

Mary Beck's eyes darted about. 'Couldn't we join another wagon, if ours gives out?'

Saul Beck took his wife's hands in his. 'All these wagons are already overloaded, honey. They'll not take on a further burden and risk their own safety.'

'But they can't leave us way out here, Saul. Mr Bassett?'

'Your husband is telling it like it is, ma'am,' Bassett confirmed. 'The load in each wagon is carefully compounded. There's not an inch of room to spare in any wagon.'

'We'll be OK, Mary,' Saul Beck told his wife. 'Calico Junction isn't much more than a good spit away.'

'Good luck, Beck. I sorely regret cutting you out, but I've got to think of the other folk in my charge.' Bassett tipped his dust-laden hat to Mary Beck. 'Ma'am.'

Dan Bassett shouted orders for the wagons behind Beck's to pull out and roll round the ailing wagon to form a new line. When the train was reorganized and about to move off, Bassett said:

'Maybe, once you get straightened out in Calico Junction, you can join the next train passing through. Most trains use the town as a stopover.

But with Indians on the prowl, I figure that it's best to reach the fort south of here as soon as possible.'

Beck nodded. 'Makes sense, I guess.'

Before rolling on, Sullivan had a change of heart and handed over a spare water canteen he had to Beck. Beck thanked him. Heavy of heart he watched the wagons depart. However, he did not delay long in turning his wagon due east.

'Next stop Calico Junction, Mary,' he said, with a confidence that did not match the hollow feeling in his gut.

Ten miles did not seem much, if they had a sound wagon, and if the Indians were not riled up by a gang of grave robbers who had raided their burial grounds for the gold adorning their dead warriors' bodies. That scurrilous deed, three weeks previously, had caused a whole heap of trouble. Wagon trains had been attacked, and some wiped out. Homesteads and ranches had suffered a similar fate. They had been lucky, as most of the Indian trouble had been behind them. But Saul Beck knew from long experience that trouble travelled fast, and he was travelling slow. Not a combination that made him rest easy.

CHAPTER TWO

Beck's progress was at a snail's pace. The trail offered a choice between sandy soil in which he might bog down, and rocky terrain whose punishment might prove too harsh for his wobbling wagon-wheel. Not long into the journey to Calico Junction, he drew rein and began unloading their belongings from the wagon.

'What are you doing, Saul?' Mary Beck enquired. 'We'll need everything we've got when we reach that free government land which we're heading for.'

Beck, worried and frustrated by the slowness of his trek, said harshly: 'The first priority is reaching Calico Junction with our hair intact, Mary.'

He swore silently as his wife's sea-blue eyes lit with alarm. He thought about trying to repair the damage his loose tongue had caused, but decided that he'd be wasting his time. Any attempt to brush over his outburst would only serve to heighten further his wife's fear.

When the wagon had been stripped down to its frame Beck climbed on board.

'Easy, hosses,' he coaxed the tired and agitated team.

He held the team back, dealing out the reins carefully. A sudden pull on the wagon might yank the damaged wheel with disastrous consequences. Beck looked out over the desert; wave after wave of shimmering heat were rising from its barren wastes. He swallowed hard. If he could, he would ditch the wagon then and there and use the team of horses to ride to Calico Junction. But bad as the jerking of the wagon was over the uneven terrain, bareback-riding a horse would likely do a lot more damage to Mary. The baby in her womb was a miracle. It was her second pregnancy following on a miscarriage which the medicos said ruled out any chance of her ever conceiving again.

For a long time after the loss of her first baby, Saul Beck had feared for Mary's sanity. He doubted very much, were she to lose the child she was now carrying, if she would survive the ordeal physically or mentally.

The well-trained team responded to Beck's caution, and eased the wagon slowly into motion. He tensed. Every rivet and plank in the wagon groaned as the damaged wheel, seeking purchase in the sandy soil, skidded and shuddered, sending out a spew of dust that rose into the still desert air; dust that might be seen by watching eyes.

He let the wagon roll back into the rut created by the spinning rear wheels, and let it settle. He jumped down to examine his degree of predicament, and how he might remedy the problem. He frowned worriedly when he saw the wagon's rear wheels deeply embedded in the soft soil, and saw no possibility of freeing them without shattering the suspect wheel.

'It's nothing, Mary,' he said, making light of his plight to ease her apprehension.

He set about gathering stones and shale to put under the wheels, hoping to give them a grip. Of course there was a risk also that rolling over the stones and shale could split the wheel anyway. However, Beck knew that since he had been kicked out of the wagon train, every minute of the journey to Calico Junction would be fraught, with the chance that each twist on the trail could bring a nasty and deadly surprise.

He helped Mary down from the wagon.

'We need every scrap of weight off that back wheel, honey.'

One last inspection of the makeshift track he had constructed satisfied Beck that he had done the best he could. He climbed on board the wagon and sat thinking for a moment. Should he give the team its head and hope that a quick and sudden jolt would do the trick? Or should he do as before, and deal out the reins an inch at the time?

In essence it was six of one and half a dozen of

the other. And only when he acted on his preferred option, would he know whether it had been the right choice.

'Here goes, Mary. Stand well back. Some of those rocks and shale might start flying. Further,' he advised, when Mary took up a position away from the wagon.

She laughed. 'Do you expect those darn rocks to reach Mexico, Saul?'

Satisfied that Mary was far enough away from danger, Beck steeled himself. He had decided to try for a sharp jolt out of trouble. He shouted: 'Yeeehhaaa!' And gave the team its head.

For a breath-stopping couple of seconds the wagon heaved and shuddered. Its boards creaked and strained. A couple of rivets popped. Saul Beck feared that the wagon would disintegrate on the spot. The crunching rear wheels spat shale in all directions. Beck held his breath.

'Come on!' he roared. 'Damn you, come on!'

Suddenly the wheels found purchase and began to roll, painful inches at first, slipping back some and then coming forward again. Sparks flew from the wheels' steel rims. A spoke on the damaged wheel snapped. Vibrations through the axle and opposite wheel sang a heart-stopping tune, before the wagon lurched forward and Saul had to rein in the team urgently to stop a headlong dash that could undo the progress made. So fierce was the wagon's release that Beck was almost unseated as

14

he tried to haul the team back, before the jolt that would surely finish the destruction of the wagon. Standing, yelling commands, Saul Beck hauled back on the reins with every smidgen of energy he could call on. Once he had control of the horses, he cooed and coaxed them to calmness until they stopped, but remained restless. He climbed down from the wagon to help his wife back on board, urging her to rest as best she could.

'Won't be long 'til we reach Calico Junction, Mary,' he reassured the frightened woman.

Grasping her husband's hand Mary Beck smiled wanly, and said unconvincingly:

'Sure it won't, Saul. No time at all, honey.'

Facing the team towards Calico Junction he prayed that he would not miss the town, which would be a mere dot in the vastness of the country. If that happened he could be headed into all sorts of trouble. The problem was that to find Calico Junction he would have to stick to the highest ground in any section of country. That meant constant danger of discovery. So all he could hope for was that any watching eyes would be friendly ones.

But so far, luck had not favoured them.

Wearily, Beck reckoned that once fickle luck deserted a man it could be slow to return.

CHAPTER THREE

As the journey to Calico Junction slowly progressed the hairs on the back of Saul Beck's neck spent more time standing than sitting. The wagon rolled and lurched, creaked and groaned, rattled and shook. The rig had taken a lot of punishment, with more to come. The scorching heat would have dried the axle and timbers, and sapped what little suppleness the ramshackle rig had had to start with. Beck listened to the wagon's every sound, trying to detect the slightest change which might hint at trouble and give him the chance to avert disaster. But he knew that in all probability the hint and the disaster would be too close for him to do anything about it. The axle, particularly, would be as brittle as dried out bone. One shudder at the wrong angle, and it would snap like a brittle twig.

He had stopped several times, hidden the wagon as best he could, and had reconnoitred the country ahead from the rocky perches. So far he had not seen a sign of Indians or anyone else. He and Mary might as well be on another planet, so bereft of company was the desolate country.

The heat of the afternoon had eventually forced him to draw rein in a shaded hollow which gave him a view of the immediate terrain around them. However, Beck knew that should trouble come, getting the wagon out of the hollow would prove almost impossible. But it was a senseless worry. The horses were spent. Needing rest, feed and water, they would not have the stamina to make any kind of fast break anyway.

Sparingly wetting a cloth, Saul moistened the horses' mouths. Saul urged Mary to drink, but the dead water made her feel sick. The groaning wagon was the lesser problem, compared to his wife's frazzled state. Another worry for Saul Beck was water. The precious commodity was in short supply. Not knowing the country, he did not know its waterholes, if there were any. And if they ran out of water, it would not be long after before they ran out of time.

'How far to go, Saul, do you reckon?' Mary Beck wearily enquired, as they shared a modest meal of jerky and biscuits. Coffee was out, due to the scarcity of water.

'Oh, I reckon not too far, honey,' Beck replied, with a casual ease that he was far from feeling.

All Saul Beck was hoping was that he had travelled in the right direction. With the desert country's uniformity of feature, a man could easily end up miles away from where he had set out for. In fact the desert was littered with the dried bones of men who had miscalculated and paid the price; men whose knowledge of the desert had been far greater than his. The desert could prove a cruel and deceptive adversary. Saul fretted over the feeling that he had traversed parts of the trail before. He could only pray that he was not going round in circles.

'You know what, Saul . . . ?'

'Hmmm?'

'I was thinking that maybe we could settle in Calico Junction.'

Beck shrugged. 'Maybe, Mary.' But rather than nurture the gleam of hope in her eyes, he cautioned: 'But I reckon that the only work round Calico Junction would be cowpunching. And that's not my line, honey.'

It hurt him to see the hope in Mary's eyes dim.

'You're not too old a dog to learn new tricks, Saul,' she said, hanging on to the last vestiges of hope. 'Can't be much difference between punching cows and planting seed, for a man with only knowledge of a gu . . .'

Mary Beck bit her tongue and averted her gaze from her husband's glare. After a long silence, Saul said, in the quite way he spoke when riled:

'I thought we agreed not to talk about my past . . . trade, Mary.'

'I'm sorry, Saul,' she sincerely apologized. 'I guess it's all this heat that's loosened my tongue and senses.'

His anger fading, Saul said: 'But you're right, of course. There's not much difference for a man who knows little about either raising cows or growing corn.' Impulsively he took his wife's hands in his.

'Except that, being a sodbuster, I'd be pretty much out of sight in that new goverment land. And out of sight means out of mind, Mary. By Bassett's description, Calico Junction doesn't amount to much, but it is a town, honey. Towns attract people – lots of people, one of whom might match my dial to a Wanted poster. And there might be men seeking to build a reputation with a gun by killing one of the fastest.'

'You're right, of course, Saul. I don't know what got into me just now, thinking that we could live like ordinary folk do.'

Saul Beck asked sincerely: 'Are you having regrets about marrying me, Mary?'

'No!'

'Because if you are, I'll ride on alone from Calico Junction.'

Her husband's questioning of her loyalty rankled, and Mary Beck asked bitterly: 'To do what? Kill more men?'

'I'm a gunfighter, Mary,' he stated bluntly. 'And that's what gunfighters do.'

Moderating her tone, Mary said: 'You hung up your gun, Saul, when you took vows.'

'Vows that don't apply if you want out, Mary.'

Suddenly weary, Mary said: 'I don't want out, Saul. But is it a crime to want peace of mind and a permanent bed to rest nights in?'

'No, it isn't. And if you'll be patient, I'll do my darnest to make that happen.' He stood up. 'Now, I reckon we should be making tracks while daylight holds.'

Saul climbed to a high ledge to scan the country ahead, and his frown of worry deepened. It was flat open country. They would be as exposed to danger as a fly crawling across an apple pie. But it pleased him too, in as much as his dire predicament would let him experience pleasure, that the far reaches of the brown and moistureless soil were beginning to show green as the desert country merged with the more fertile range of cow country. It would take a couple of hours more, once the margins of the desert were reached, to roll through the rich grass-lands needed to fatten stock. But it was surely an indicator that he was on course for Calico Junction. Or at least for civilization.

Saul Beck's nerves were just losing their rawness when he heard Mary's scream. Alarmed, he swung around, almost losing his footing on the narrow ledge. Despite the heat of the afternoon, his blood ran cold.

CHAPTER FOUR

The Apache was standing over Mary. His stance, a straddling one, signalled his intentions. What puzzled Beck was the Indian's brazenness. The Apache must have seen him climb to the ledge, and had had ample time to pick him off with the shiny new rifle he held across his chest. So why had he not done so? The answer to the Indian's bravado was delivered when, from overhead, a fistful of shale clattered down on Beck's shoulders. Just as he glanced up a second Indian was dropping down on him, a long-bladed hunting-knife reflecting the glint of the sun. So intense was the reflection that Saul, dazzled, lost precious seconds in taking counter measures against the threat of imminent death. The ledge was a narrow, thin strip of rock that offered precious little leeway for a man to dodge. A couple of inches either way could send Saul plummeting to the rocky base of the ledge. And it was likely that if the dropping Indian landed on him, the momentum would pitch both men over the edge.

Saul dropped on to his back and extended his legs upwards. He had gambled well. The Apache crashed down on to his legs. Beck screamed out with the pressure pains shooting into his hips and belly. His spine, too, reverberated with the shock of the Indian's weight. But his pain was worth it when the Apache spun off his legs and, with a shriek of terror vanished over the edge of the ledge. Seconds later, the crunch of breaking bones filled the afternoon stillness.

A bullet buzzed past Beck's face and corkscrewed back off the rockface, clipping the lobe of his right ear. He felt a gush of hot blood stream down his neck. He rolled over and made himself as flat a target as he could on the virtually coverless ledge. Lying flat on his belly would make it difficult for the Indian below to get in a killing shot. He would have to climb a little higher than the flat ground around the hollow he had Mary trapped in to make the shot, and Beck was hoping that the concentration the Apache would have to put in to pick his way through the rocks safely would, at some point, present him with the opportunity to pick him off.

That was the plan, and it was the best that Saul Beck could do with only a six-gun to counter the Indian's rifle. There was also the possibility that lurking above him or in the rocks around the ledge, there could be other Indians. But Beck was counting on there not being any, figuring that if there were they would have shown their hand to diminish the risk to the Apache holding Mary prisoner. Also, Apaches being hot-blooded, Beck reckoned that their reaction to his crafty dispatch of their comrade would have brought an instant response. All he could hope for in the next couple of minutes was that his reasoning had a basis of common sense, rather the fanciful desperation of a man with the odds stacked against him.

The Apache moved with the speed of a mountain cat and the craftiness of a man in tune with his environment. The Indian's knowledge of the terrain was an advantage that was worth its weight in gold to him. However, what was gold to the Apache was a millstone round Saul Beck's neck.

Despite the Indian's slick but cagey movement upwards through the rocks, a couple of half-chances for Saul to try and pick him off were presented to him. But he held his fire, awaiting something more than a fleeting glimpse of the Apache to nail him.

It was hard to remain patient, but he had to curb the urge to take a risk, and could only shoot when he had more than a fifty/fifty chance of killing the Indian, or at least maiming him to a degree that made him no threat to his or Mary's well-being. He had feared that the Apache would force him out by using Mary as a hostage, but obviously the Indian reckoned that he could deal with him without risking injury to Mary. Because she was the prize that was at stake. A weak man, insane with the fear of Apache torture, might just shoot through the woman to kill the Indian. She might be a passing stranger upon whom Beck placed no value, and would have no hesitation in sacrificing her to save his own hide.

Beck was sure, too, that the Apache had spotted his rifle on the seat of the wagon where he had left it, and he would know that his opponent would need a whacking great dollop of luck for him to get an accurate shot off with a six-gun, until he was knocking on his door.

When Mary Stratton had accepted his proposal of marriage, Saul had promised that he would never again buckle on a gunbelt – a promise he had kept. But now it was a promise that could backfire horribly on them both. The six-gun tucked inside the waist of his trousers was short two rounds. If he had been wearing a gunbelt, his stock of bullets would be healthier by far.

He had four bullets to deal with the Indian. A gun that close up was lethal, but very uncertain at distance. It was not a happy position to be in.

Steadily, the Apache climbed. Beck reckoned that his best chance to down the Indian would come when he had to cross the narrow strip of open ground that separated the lower rocks from those higher up, which he would have to gain to make a telling shot. However, Beck knew that once he took that chance, his gunfire could bring him more trouble than he already had. The risk was that the Apaches were not just two strays, but were either forward or back trail scouts. His gunfire could bring a whole horde of Indians charging.

Saul Beck's thoughts were not for himself, but for Mary. Blue eyes, yellow hair, skin as smooth and blemish-free as Wisconsin cream. He shuddered. Cold in the intense heat of the desert. He knew that his and Mary's chances of slipping free of the Indians' clutches were almost zero. And even if they had the luck of a leprechaun, they would have to make their escape on foot, hoping to hide until the Apaches tired of the chase or night fell. Beck would be the first to admit that he was not an expert in the ways of the Apache, but he sincerely hoped that the stories told him about Apache reluctance to fight at night were true.

He saw dust on the horizon. Beck peered into the sun and his blood ran cold. The main war party! Not too far off, but maybe far enough to give them a chance to escape, but he would have to deal with the Indian in the next couple of minutes.

The Apache, too, had seen the dust trail. And confident that there was no way out for the white man and his woman, he made Saul Beck a proposition.

'White eyes,' he hailed. 'Go. Leave your woman.'

Seething, Saul Beck shouted back:

'Go rot in hell, you stinking bastard!'

CHAPTER FIVE

Beck had no choice but to throw caution to the wind. He sprinted along the ledge in an attempt to reach an overhang that would offer him protection, and at the same time place him at a difficult shooting angle for the Indian. Bullets buzzed round him, ricocheting off the rockface. Shooting a moving target was never easy. For the Apache, whose use of a repeater rifle was a recently acquired skill, impossible. But there was always the chance of a lucky shot.

As he ran, Saul Beck saw his wife making tracks for the wagon, presumably to get hold of the Winchester. Mary Beck had seldom held a rifle, let alone used one. But if she could manage to fire the rifle and distract the Indian, because he would not know how little a threat Mary was, it might give him a chance to sneak out from under the overhang and blast the Apache to Hades.

Beck held his breath as Mary's foot caught on her dress and she stumbled headlong. He cut loose with a round to occupy the Indian's concentration. It worked. Because, as luck would have it, the speculative shot grazed the Indian's left arm. Meanwhile, Mary was on her feet again and running openly for the wagon and the rifle hidden there. Another round from Beck was necessary to give Mary any chance of making it. That left him with only two bullets. And if his wife's desperate attempt to even the score failed, two bullets would not be enough to deal with the Indian.

Then Saul Beck changed his mind. He had only one bullet left. Because of the two in the six-gun's chamber, he would use one on Mary to save her from the horror she would face when the main war party showed up.

The Apache, nursing his wounded arm, turned his attention to Mary Beck. She had reached the wagon and was reaching for the Winchester. The rifle was in her grasp. She spun round and fired the gun. It clicked hollowly, as the old weapon misfired. Panicked, she fumbled with the rifle. Beck held his breath. Fumbling with a contrary rifle was not a smart thing to do. The rifle fell from her grasp and clattered to the ground. There would be no time to retrieve the weapon. The Indian was lining her up in his sights.

'Duck, Mary!' Saul shouted.

Confused and panicked, Mary froze. She stood stock still, offering herself as an easy target.

Beck fired and wasted his last bullet.

The explosion of the six-gun snapped Mary Beck out of her fear-induced trance. She had the presence of mind to retrieve the Winchester before sprinting behind a small boulder which did not offer much cover, but any more substantial a hiding-place was either too close to the Apache, or too far away to safely make for.

Beck's bullet had instilled a sense of caution in the Indian, which gave Mary the seconds she needed to get out of his gun sights. So he consoled himself that the precious round was not completely wasted.

Mary triggered the rifle again and the weapon fired. The shot was hopelessly wild and posed a greater danger to Saul than to the Indian, but the distraction handed Beck a clear opportunity when the Apache, diving for cover, stumbled and fell forward from his hidy-hole to lie on open ground. Beck had a split-second in which to decide whether he should use his truly last bullet to try and kill the Indian. If he failed the Apache would have a free hand, and Mary's ordeal would only be beginning.

By now the Indian would have realized how wild Mary's shot had been, and would therefore know that she was a greenhorn when it came to the use of a rifle. And, cunning as Apaches were, in the absence of gunfire from Beck it would not take the Indian much longer to realize that Saul was short on lead.

31

As the Indian scrambled back to cover, Beck fired. The length of time it took for the bullet to travel the distance to the Indian seemed eternal. The Apache jerked and grabbed his left side. Blood showed where the bullet had, Beck reckoned, smashed a couple of ribs.

The Apache was maimed but still lethal.

The Indian's fury was etched in every line of his face. If they were to have any chance of survival, Saul Beck had to get his hands on his rifle.

Now it was all or nothing.

He leaped from the ledge, aiming to land in a patch of sandy soil far below to absorb his fall. But, impulsive and ill-prepared as his leap had been, it looked as though he would miss the sandy soil and crash into the rocks just short of safety. That, if he survived at all, would leave him with many broken bones. And even if the Indian was mortally wounded, it would leave Mary on her own and helpless to face the oncoming war party.

A painful brush with a stunted tree growing out of the rockface like a cancer changed the direction of Beck's fall and he landed at the edge of the patch of sandy soil, bones jarred but intact. Ignoring the pain of his jolted spine, he ran towards Mary.

'Throw me the rifle, Mary!' he shouted.

The Winchester sailed through the air. Saul had to reach for it and almost missed it, his outstretched fingers barely grabbing the rifle's barrel as it flashed past. He flicked the rifle and pulled the trigger in one fluid movement, the way a man used to handling guns can. The Winchester spat twice. The Apache's face exploded. He was lifted off his feet and tossed back into the rocks.

Mary ran to her husband, wanting the comfort of his arms. His comforting was brief. He hurried her to cover. Seconds later the war party put in an appearance.

CHAPTER SIX

'Stay put!' Beck ordered, pulling Mary back down as fear would have put her to flight. 'And remain perfectly still, Mary.'

Breathless, she said, 'They'll smell our scent like the animals they are, Saul.'

'No, they won't,' Beck said, wishing that the positive rebuff of his wife's opinion held more inner conviction than its verbalization. The war party would know that they could not have gone far. As the Indians chattered excitedly, Saul Beck wished that he knew Apache lingo. However, his lack of knowledge was no impediment to understanding the angry exchanges. The leader of the war party barked orders. The Apaches dismounted and fanned out into the rocks.

Mary Beck gripped her husband's hand and wept.

'We're done for, Saul.'

Grim-faced, Saul said, 'Not yet.' He patted the rifle.

On the verge of hysteria, Mary dismissed the importance of the Winchester.

'They'll be all over us,' Saul,' she wailed. 'We don't stand a chance. They'll butcher us both!'

There was nothing Beck could say to convince her otherwise, or indeed himself either. He had counted twelve Indians. There would be more, he reckoned, higher up, to give covering fire to the Indians who had ridden in. Though the Apache was perceived by white men as being more a spirited than a strategic fighter, all the evidence of their battles, often against overwhelming and superiorly armed opponets, showed that they were no fools.

Saul Beck figured that they had come to the end of a trail of hope that had begun the day when Mary Stratton, as she then was, stepped into the Pennington stage in a way station called Crooked Creek.

Beck's mind drifted back to that day . . . .

'My, but it's hot, isn't it?' Mary had said, fanning herself with her bonnet.

'Surely is,' Saul had replied, readily giving up his window seat to her. 'Once we get going,' he promised, 'there will be a nice breeze on your face.'

'Oh, but I can't take your seat, sir,' Mary had protested. 'It wouldn't be fair.'

'It won't give me any pleasure to see you wilt on a centre seat, ma'am,' Saul had said.

'Well,' Mary's smile had been devasting. 'In that

case . . .'

Mary accepted Beck's offer and, seated by the window, the wind blowing her corn-coloured hair across her face, Saul had never seen such beauty before. Going his wandering way, he had met and sought the pleasure of many women, but never had he gleaned such pleasure from just sitting, watching the woman he had given his seat to. Two other men in the coach were equally enchanted by Mary Stratton. Two female passengers on board were openly hostile, as women are to other women who have the ability to charm men in such a thrilling and spellbinding fashion.

'Might I ask your destination, ma'am?' one of the men, portly and red-faced, enquired.

'Pennington, sir,' Mary replied.

'Pennington, huh?' the second man said, his calloused hands showing his profession to be that of a rancher or farmer, as opposed to the portly man's soft-skinned hands that told of a profession which was more cerebral than manual. Perhaps a banker or lawyer. 'Small, but it's got the makings of a fine town some day.'

'But a tad raw as yet, ma'am. 'Til tough law settles it down.'

'We've got a sheriff, Watts.'

The man called Watts scoffed.

'Sam Murphy? Might as well have a darn ghost wearing a badge.'

'That new deputy is on his way,' the portly man

said. Fast as rattler, I hear. Used to be a gunfighter.'

At this point, Saul Beck had sat up from his slouched position, fast-drawing lawmen being of intense interest to him. Particularly a former gunfighter who had become a badge-toter.

'Has this new deputy got a name?' he enquired of his fellow passengers.

'Why, mister?' Watts asked.

'Are you going to Pennington, too?' one of the women, a shrewish specimen, asked Beck. Her glance went; not for the first time, to the low-slung six-gun on Saul Beck's right hip.

'Yes. As a matter of fact, I am,' Beck said.

'Business in Pennington, have you?' the second woman, dressed in widow's weeds, asked, her gaze, like the other woman's, sliding to Beck's .45.

'Maybe.'

Mary Stratton enquired: 'Travelled far?'

'From Louis Crossing.'

'Would that be Louis Crossing in Texas?' Mary asked.

Beck had grinned. 'You know your geography, ma'am,' he complimented.

'I'm a teacher.'

'Pennington's new teacher?' the portly man enquired of Mary.

'Yes.'

'Lucas Braden.' He introduced himself. 'President of the Pennington Bank. At your service, Miss . . . ?'

'Stratton. Mary Stratton.'

'The town can sure do with a good teacher,' Watts declared. He shook Mary's hand. 'Tom Watts. Farm 'bout five miles south of town.' His shoulders slumped. 'If that cur Rufe Thomas don't run me out, like he's done most of my neighbours.'

'Hear that Thomas has hired a gunfighter, Braden. You hear that?'

'It seems so,' Braden said. 'I don't know if I can blame him, Tom. Rufe's a good friend of mine, and he's had a lot of trouble with nesters.'

'I ain't no nester!' Watts growled.

'Didn't say you were, Tom,' the banker soothed. 'But Colonel Thomas needs more range for that ever-growing herd of his—'

'Farmers have rights too,' Watts said, his attitude uncompromising. 'Like the right to not have cows trampling their crops.'

'Sure they have,' the banker conceded. 'But Pennington is cow country, Tom. And cows and crops just don't mix.'

'Ev'ry man's got a right to make a crust as best he knows how,' was Tom Watts's steely stand.

The shrewish woman said, her comments directed at Watts:

'All I know is that without Colonel Thomas's enterprise, Pennington would not have the railhead which it now has. A town with a railhead can only grow and become more prosperous.'

'Yes,' the other woman put in. 'Without the

Thomas ranch and that railhead we wouldn't have that fine new school which Miss Stratton will be teaching in.'

It was clear to Saul Beck that Watts, and presumably the other farmers round Pennington, were about as popular as lepers.

Braden said, 'I don't agree with the town council hiring that fellow Barton as Murphy's deputy. Rufe's crew aren't really doing any harm.'

'Terrorizing and burning folk out of their homes ain't no harm?' Watts had raged.

'Rufe's made each and every farmer a fair offer for his land.' Braden defended the rancher.

'Don't agree 'bout it bein' a fair offer, Braden,' Watts argued. 'But even if it was a fair offer, it's only fair if a man wants to move on.' He said with grim finality, 'I ain't never goin' to up roots at the barrel of a gun!'

The banker shrugged. 'You can't stop progress, Tom. You should accept Rufe Thomas's offer. Why he'll even give you a job as a cowpuncher if you want it.'

'Would that be Hal Barton?' Saul Beck asked, during a lull in the argument.

'Yes,' Tom Watts confirmed. 'A former gunslinger who now hires himself out as a badge-toter to towns where law and order's broken down. Best damn thing the town council's ever done, I say.'

'It would be,' Lucas Braden agreed, 'if law and order had broken down. Rufe running off a few troublesome nest . . . farmers,' he hastily amended under Watts's fiery glare, 'isn't exactly law and order breaking down.'

Mary Stratton said to Beck, 'You've come a long way for a man who's not sure if he has or has not got business to conduct in Pennington?'

'Sometimes, ma'am,' Beck had said, 'a whole passel of things can change between a man starting out on a journey and its end.'

Saul recalled how true that statement had been. Because he had already decided that he would reject Rufe Thomas's killer's bounty to do his dirty work for him. And the reason for his conversion was sitting across the stagecoach from him: Pennington's new schoolmarm. Who, he had decided, would be his wife. And if she was not, then it would not be from a lack of effort on his part.

'Staying long?' Tom Watts asked the question, but had already decided on the answer. 'You wouldn't be a guest of Rufe Thomas, would you?'

'I'll be parleying with that gent, yes,' Beck had replied.

'Then I guess,' Watts said, sourly, 'if you're planning on hitching your wagon to the colonel's outfit, it explains that rig on your hip. Who's Thomas planning on running out now?'

It concerned Beck that the young woman he had given his seat to was beginning to look at him in a way that was familiar when folk found out that he was a gunfighter.

41

For Mary Stratton's part, being a gunfighter was the very last profession she would have slotted him in to.

'You look more like a doctor, or . . . maybe a preacher,' she had later told him.

Beck had smiled. 'Look, mister. I admit that I had been planning on hiring out to Colonel Thomas. But,' Saul's eyes had settled on Mary Stratton, 'like I said, a whole passel of things can change from when a man starts out on a journey and its end.'

He held Mary Stratton's gaze until she was forced to look away.

'Oh, you'll accept Rufe Thomas's dollars all right,' Watts opined bitterly. 'Men like you aren't interested in the rights and wrongs of what men like Rufe Thomas do. Your only interest is in lining your pockets with his killer's bounty.'

The farmer snorted.

'But I figure that Hal Barton will have your measure, mister. And the sooner the better, I say.'

'Are you acquainted with Mr Barton?' Lucas Braden enquired of Beck.

'I know the gent,' Saul had admitted.

Hal Barton was a tough-as-nails former gunfighter who had become a free-lance lawman, hiring out to towns who were fighting corruption and tyranny. When Barton's work was done he upped and moved on. And Hal Barton towns had acquired a reputation as towns that had extremely busy undertakers.

With steel-tough lawmen such as Rangers and US marshals, and an equally flinty judiciary, life had become a lot tamer, and tame times meant lean pickings for men who earned their living by their fast draw.

Barton, a clever *hombre*, had found a way to operate, in essence, as a gunfighter, but with the legality of a badge. Maybe, Saul had pondered on that final couple of miles to Pennington on the day that was to change his life, if he could not persuade the new schoolmarm to be his bride, following in Hal Barton's footsteps might be the way to go.

But as it turned out, three weeks after their arrival in Pennington, Mary Stratton had agreed to walk out with him.

'But only if you come calling without that!'

She had pointed to Saul's six-gun.

Then and there Beck had gladly and willingly unbuckled his gunbelt.

Saul Beck forced his mind back to the present. His mood was one of melancholy. He had dared to dream that he could hang up his gun and make a life with Mary as new homesteaders. Now that dream was about to vanish. But he supposed that it was a dream that had not stood much of a chance from the start. He cursed the moonlit night he had asked Mary to be his wife, and had pitched her into the wayward life which had been her lot since.

'It won't be easy, Mary,' he had told her.

Mary had held him fiercely. 'I know it won't, Saul,' she'd whispered. 'But I'm willing to try, if you are?'

Hell, was he willing to try!

He further cautioned: 'A reputation with a fast gun can come back to haunt a man when he might least expect it to.'

'Well, Saul,' she had said with schoolmarm practicality, 'we'll just have to learn to live one day at a time.'

He had arrived in Pennington to be met at the stage depot by Colonel Rufe Thomas, who immediately escorted him to his home for a fine meal and all he could drink. The dining-room, indeed most rooms in the house, were flush with the photographs and mementeos of war with which Thomas regaled his visitors.

Then, wined and dined, Thomas had figured that Saul Beck was in a frame of mind for straight talking. It was a familiar conversation. When a man hired a gunfighter, it was for only one reason. He needed a fast draw to further his own ambitions, and Rufe Thomas was no different from the others Saul Beck had served. The usual litany of obstacles to Thomas's expansionary plans in both ranching and town business ventures were trotted out, and the colonel made it quite clear that the removal of these obstacles would bring handsome rewards for Beck.

'I'm a generous man to those who do my bidding, Beck,' he'd told Saul. 'When your work here in Pennington is finished,' he grinned, 'and it's up to you how soon that might be, you'll be riding on with a poke that you never dreamed you'd have.'

Thomas put a thousand dollars on the table.

'And that's just a down payment.'

Beck had not reached for the bills.

Perplexed, Thomas had coaxed: 'Feel those bills between your fingers, Beck. And think about how thick that wad can grow.'

Beck still did not pick up Thomas's dollars.

His jovial mood sliding, the colonel growled surlily: 'Something wrong with my money?'

'No, Colonel, there's nothing wrong with your money,' Beck said. 'You see, my priorities have changed on the journey here . . .'

Thomas scoffed. 'Changed? You're the first gunfighter I've known who didn't grab my money, Beck. What's the reason for your reticence?'

'I plan on getting married.'

'Married!' Rufe Thomas was aghast.

'Yes, sir. I intend to make the new schoolteacher my wife.'

'Schoolteacher, huh?' The colonel's tone was openly derisive. 'And what schoolteacher would marry a damn gunfighter?'

'Well,' Beck sighed, 'Miss Mary Stratton, I hope.'

Since it had been revealed on the stage that he was a gunfighter, Mary's attitude towards him had cooled. This greatly perturbed him. Her reaction, of course, was not new. He had experienced it a hundred times before. It would be Thomas's reaction, too, once he had done his dirty work for him. To decent folk, not that he'd put Rufe Thomas in that bracket, gunfighters were lepers. And that fact had not unduly troubled Beck until he had fallen in love with Mary Stratton.

Rufe Thomas's attitude was typical of men to whom all women had but one purpose.

'Pretty as a picture, is our new schoolmarm, sure enough. But then the town saloons are full of pretty women, and you won't have to marry them to get them between the sheets.' Thomas snorted.

'Your kind of women, Beck. Women who've got more tricks than a damn magician!'

Another man might have taken exception to Thomas's remarks. But Saul Beck was honest enough to recognize the former man he had been in the colonel's assessment, and was equally ready to accept that Rufe Thomas's thinking was based on the norm for men of his kind, and had not been purposely malicious.

'Now, Lazy Lil, over at the Wagon Wheel saloon.' He rolled his eyes. 'There's a gal! We call her Lazy Lil because she spends most of her day and night on her back.' He paused, before offering: 'Now if you want an introduction . . . ?'

Beck stood up. 'I thank you for the grub. And

I'm sorry for wasting your time, too. But I'm not your man, Colonel.'

'Not my man!' Thomas flared. 'You're acting kind of uppity for a two-bit gunslinger, aren't you?' He said contemptuously: 'Do you honestly think that our new and lovely schoolteacher is going to give you, a gunfighter, a second glance?'

'I won't be a gunslinger when I court her, Colonel. That's why I'm refusing your money.'

Rufe Thomas sized up Saul, and his contempt deepened.

'It's Hal Barton, isn't it. You're scared of going up against Hal Barton,' he taunted. 'Afraid of finding out who's faster. There's been a whole lot of talk about that. And I reckon that now we'll never know, will we? Because your tail's between your legs, Beck.'

Beck stated honestly: 'A man would be a fool to ignore Hal Barton's ability with a gun, Colonel. Such stupidity has filled a lot of graves. But Barton doesn't figure in my rejection of your dollars. Thing is, packing a six-gun, Mary Stratton won't come closer to me than the moon.'

Since he had set eyes on Mary, the gun on his hip felt alien and he wanted rid of it. He just hoped that trading his gun for Mary Stratton's affection, would get the divine blessing it would need to succeed.

Beck said, 'I'm sure that you'll have no difficulty in replacing me, Colonel.'

Rufe Thomas's bitter threat trailed him out of the house.

'I won't, Beck. And his first job will be to track you down and kill you. No man refuses or defies Rufe Thomas and gets away with it!'

Arriving back in town, he spotted Mary Stratton strolling along the boardwalk, and he cheekily fell in alongside her.

'I don't recall issuing you with an invitation to walk with me, Mr Beck,' Mary had said, starchily.

'No, ma'am,' Beck said. 'But I aim to walk alongside you quite a bit in the future.'

She paused, her sea-blue eyes twinkling mischievously.

'Is that so?'

'That's so, Miss Stratton,' Saul told Pennington's new teacher.

'I might have something to say about that, Mr Beck.'

'I reckon you will. A whole lot, I'd imagine. But . . .'

'But?'

'Well,' Beck said determinedly, 'I know that I'm heading for a whole passel of brickbats, Mary. And I'm sure there'll be times when you'll be angry, and times when you'll be downright rude. But I intend to hang around until you agree to become Mrs Saul Beck.'

When Mary had got over her astonishement, she had laughed heartily.

'You do say, Mr Beck?'

'Yes, I do, ma'am.'

'Then,' Mary Stratton had concluded, 'you might not know it, but I reckon that one of those bullets you've been dodging got inside your head, Mr Beck.'

Cheekily, he had replied, 'That'll be Saul, Mary.'

Mary flung back, 'And that will be Miss Stratton, Mr Beck.'

As she strode away, Saul had promised: 'I'll be paying my respects soon, Mary.'

Beck fought back the anguish at what had been inevitable since the first Indians had put in an appearance, and probably from the second they were forced out of the wagon train in country teeming with threat and menace.

'Check that side, Mary,' he said, pointing to a direction in which her back would be to him, because he simply could not look her in the face when he triggered the Winchester.

Over time Saul Beck had often regretted having wooed Mary Stratton. If he had not so relentlessly and single-mindedly pursued her she would now be safe in Pennington, and probably married to a man who did not have to keep looking over his shoulder all the time. Comfortable in her own home, instead of squatting in dirt and grime. Not for the first time, Beck knew he had gravely wronged her by inflicting on her a way of life that she did not deserve.

Levelling the Winchester, he murmured, 'Sorry, Mary.'

The trigger of the Winchester was half-depressed when a volley of rifle shots erupted from a ridge, which was the highest point in the arid landscape. As Indians tumbled from their horses, Mary's eyes lit with delight.

'We're saved, Saul,' she yelled.

Saved? Were they?

Saul could not see the shooters. But they were close enough to the Mexican border for Mex bandits to make a foray. And there was also the possibility of gangs who would know, like the Mexicans, that across the border a Mexican whorehouse would pay top dollar for a woman as beautiful as Mary Beck. Beck knew that when the shooting was over and the dust settled, he might be faced with exactly the same problem that Mary thought they'd just ditched.

As the few Apaches who had survived the blistering gunfire galloped off, Saul restrained his wife's glee, keeping her down when she wanted to jump up to welcome their rescuers.

'Best to wait, Mary,' he told her.

She did not ask why. Because now she too was beginning to understand that the removal of the Apache threat to their safety might only herald even greater danger.

CHAPTER SEVEN

The minutes ticked by. No one showed on the ridge.

'They're just being cautious, honey,' Beck told his wife to ease her fretting. 'Indians are cunning critters. They could double back.'

'Yes. That must be why they're staying put, I guess,' Mary said breathlessly.

More time dragged by.

'Maybe they're gone, Saul?'

'I guess that could be it,' Beck consoled his wife, not believing for a second that it was the case.

Soon after his first thoughts were confirmed. The visitors' guns opened up to kill three Apaches creeping up on them from behind. This was followed by an eerie stillness and more waiting. At last:

'Howdy, down there!'

Saul Beck looked up at the tall man on top of the ridge who was waving to them. At least he was white. American. Too well-turned-out to be a bandit. Other men were standing up to join him – six in all. Saul returned his greeting.

'Howdy.'

'Calico's the name, mister,' the tall, grey-eyed man introduced himself on coming to greet Saul and Mary. 'John Calico. I boss the Circle C over Calico Junction way. Finest darn ranch in these parts, I reckon.'

Beck returned John Calico's firm and friendly handshake.

'Saul and Mary Beck. My wife and I thank you and your men for putting legs under those Apaches. It didn't seem likely that we'd see tomorrow before you happened along.'

Most of the Calico crew scrambled down through the rocks from the ridge to meet Saul and Mary. Two men remained on the ridge.

'You fellas keep your eyes peeled,' Calico instructed the men. 'Just in case there are more of those varmints lurking.'

The rancher tipped his hat respectfully to Mary. 'You and your man have had a lucky escape, ma'am.' His next comments were addressed to Saul: 'What the devil were you thinking about, setting off alone in Indian country?' But there was more sympathy for a fool than rebuke in his tone. 'No country at all for a woman with Apaches on the prowl.'

Saul Beck did not take umbrage, because he figured that if his and Calico's positions were reversed, he'd be every bit as critical.

Mary Beck sprang to her man's defence.

'We were part of a wagon train, Mr Calico. Our wagon was creaking, and we were forced out.'

Calico's glance went to the Becks' crumbling wagon.

'If you don't mind me saying so, ma'am,' the rancher opined, 'that wagon was in no fit condition starting out to begin with.'

It was firmly established by now that John Calico was a man who liked blunt speech. Saul Beck had no quibble with that. He wasn't exactly a diplomat himself.

'Maybe that's true, sir,' Mary said curtly. 'And I dare say that you can afford better. But that was the best wagon that Saul and I could afford.'

The rancher shifted uneasily under Mary Beck's fiery gaze. Some of the men behind him put their hands over their mouths to hide their smiles. A couple showed their mirth in the shake of their shoulders. Obviously they were not used to hearing their boss dressed down in so brisk a fashion, and probably not at all by a woman.

John Calico swung round, flinty eyes sweeping the Circle C crew in a silent reprimand that stilled the men's mirth.

Saul said, 'You sure twigged a nerve in Mary, Mr Calico.'

Calico said sheepishly, 'Didn't mean no critcism ma'am.' Then he corrected under Mary Beck's steady gaze. 'Well, I guess I did at that. But it was of your man rather than you, Mrs Beck.'

'My man, Mr Calico, did the best he could. And if that's good enough for me, then I don't see why it shouldn't be good enough for you.'

This time there were no smiles on the Calico crew's faces. They had never heard anyone talk with such forthrightness to their boss before, and knew that he had horsewhipped men for a whole lot less. It brought stark looks of awe to their faces when John Calico laughed heartily, it being the reaction that they had not even remotely expected from the stern rancher.

'Mrs Beck, ma'am,' he chuckled, 'you've got the spit of a fine stallion.'

'Mare, Mr Calico,' Mary said.

'As you'll have gathered, ma'am,' his gaze rested on the gob-smacked crew, 'the kind of lip you've dished out is something which I'm not use to getting, or,' his voice dropped a notch, 'taking . . .'

'From any man?' Mary suggested in the rancher's pause.

'Yes, ma'am.'

'Well, if you've got something to say, or do,' Mary said, 'don't let my skirts get in your way of doing it, Mr Calico.'

Saul Beck feared that Mary had gone too far, and was beginning to regret not leashing her in when he saw the red line of anger rise above John Calico's collar. Not that, from experience, trying to leash her in would not have made Mary any less stubborn.

Calico looked squarely at Beck, expecting him to rein Mary in. In a country where women had little say and less sway, it was expected of a man to control the woman in his charge.

Beck said, with a widening grin, 'You've ruffled a she-cat, Mr Calico. I figure that it's your job to unruffle her.'

'That a fact!' Calico blustered. 'Do you always give your woman so much rope, Beck?'

Saul chuckled. 'It's not a matter of my giving, Calico. Mary cuts her own length.'

'I'll be damned!' the rancher swore. He swung Mary Beck's way, his anger dissipated and replaced by a hearty sense of amusement. 'Before you know it, men,' he said, 'we'll have female range bosses, if this spirited woman gets her way.'

Mary said, 'I hope they'll know their genders better than you appear to do, Mr Calico.'

'Mrs Beck, ma'am?'

'Seeing that you don't seem to know the difference between a stallion and a mare.'

This time there was no holding back on the crew's laughter – all except one man whom Saul had seen sulkily hanging back from the main body of the crew. And it was not hard to peg him as John Calico's seed. The same slant of jawline, same gait and dark hair. But it was the eyes wherein the difference between the men lay. Calico senior had grey eyes, the same as Calico junior, but in junior's eyes there was a soullessness that was not in John Calico's eyes. Saul Beck reckoned that the men, who looked so like each other in appearance, were in fact poles apart in heart and spirit.

Beck, having had time to study John Calico, had his first impression of having met the man before strengthened. But where could their paths have crossed?

'I don't see anything to laugh about,' Calico junior said coldly. The crew's laughter staggered, caught as they were between loyalties. 'I figure no woman,' now his glance went to Saul Beck, 'or man, should talk to a Calico with such brashness, Pa.'

The elder Calico said, 'Mrs Beck meant no insolence, Tod. And I found it refreshing that a woman should hold such firm views.'

'I didn't,' Tod Calico growled. 'And you should have contolled your wife's utterances, mister,' he told Saul Beck.

Beck, riled by Tod Calico's mean attitude, responded curtly:

'I don't rightly see that you or I had any say in what passed between your father and my wife, Calico. So their gab is their business, I reckon.'

Tod Calico stepped forward. A pathway between Calico's men instantly opened up for him, in a way that told Saul Beck that the men were following a familiar routine.

'That'll be *Mister* Calico to you,' Tod snarled.

'I don't want any trouble,' Beck said, his voice not much above a whisper. 'I've had more than a bellyful.'

'Then,' Tod Calico sneered, and took up a stance that Beck recognized. The men behind him drifted to either side of him in a familiar pattern. 'You tell your wife to apologize to my pa and me.'

Mary Beck, keenly aware of how ugly a turn the mood had taken, was about to utter the apology which Tod Calico had demanded. It would go against the grain for her to have to apologize, but it would be better than letting the brewing trouble reach boiling point. If that happened, and Saul had to face Tod Calico, she reckoned that there could only be one winner. Tod Calico would eat dust. And Saul's swiftness with a six-gun, a secret they had worked hard to keep, would be revealed. After that the inevitable questions would follow, about how a man with a beat up wagon heading for free government land, was so gun-slick. It would not take too long for the picture to be completed and Saul's gunslinger's past would be revealed, with all the trouble that would follow his unmasking.

Saul put his hand to his wife's lips to still her apology. He told her:

'You had your say, Mary. That you're entitled to.' He turned back to Tod Calico. 'I've got an empty six-gun, Calico. But it will only take me a couple of seconds to put that right; seconds you should use to think carefully, son.'

Tod Calico scoffed. 'There ain't nothing to think about, Beck.' He ordered the man nearest to him, a slimy example of the species, 'Bud, sling him your gunbelt.'

The man willingly obliged. Bud's gunbelt fell at Saul Beck's feet.

Though John Calico did not approve of his son's readiness to settle every dispute with a gun, a trait that would one day be his undoing if he did not curb his impetuosity, he did not intervene. He was frankly curious. Was Saul Beck bluffing? Would he cave in once gunplay became inevitable? The rancher would not let his son draw on Beck. His intervention would be timely, if the confrontation developed to the point of a killing.

Beck picked up the gunbelt. He buckled it on. He rolled the gun's chamber. Six bullets. He balanced the .45 in the palm of his right hand, testing its weight, getting its feel. He curled his finger round the trigger and tested its spring. He holstered the six-gun, looked Tod Calico in the eye, and said:

'I don't want this, son. My advice is that you back off.'

Tod Calico looked to Mary Beck and sneered.

'You're about to become a widow, ma'am.'

The sudden cold sweat breaking on John Calico told him different. He had watched Saul Beck closely, and had recognized in his careful and calm preparation the mark of a man who knew what he was about. He was not bluffing, or driven by foolish pride. He would not cave in either. And Mary Beck, the rancher was convinced, would not be a widow as Tod had predicted. Instead it was probable that he would lose a son and heir. If Tod bit the dust, there would be no one left to pass on the fruits of his labour to. Tod was not the calibre of man he would have wanted for a son, but he was his seed.

He had also expected to see in Saul Beck's face the grey pallor of a man who had stupidly over-played his hand. His expectation had not materi-alized. Beck's eyes held the steely resolve of a man confident in the knowledge that the task to be completed was well within his remit.

Tod Calico sniggered.

'Ready, Beck? I wouldn't want anyone saying that I didn't give you a fair chance.'

Beck looked to John Calico.

'This is not of my making, Mr Calico. Be mind-ful of that.' He turned to Tod Calico. 'You call it, son,' he said.

John Calico knew that Tod was seconds away from death.

'Hold it, Tod!' he ordered. 'This brinkmanship has gone far enough.'

'Are you asking me to back down, Pa?' Tod Calico growled.

'Telling,' came the rancher's brusque reply.

Tod Calico's eyes danced dangerously. 'I figure that you should be telling Beck, 'stead of me, Pa.'

'I said to stop this nonsense right now, Tod,' John Calico barked.

'If Beck begs, I will,' Tod Calico said, his defiance absolute. 'Are you begging, Beck?'

Saul Beck's stance made it obvious that he was not.

'Saul . . .' There was deep and desperate pleading in Mary Beck's voice.

Beck swallowed hard. 'I guess I am, Calico,' he murmured.

'That'll be *Mister* Calico,' the rancher's son demanded.

'Mister Calico,' Beck said, his lips set in a thin line.

Tod Calico cocked an ear. 'What was that? You're mumbling, Beck.'

'That's enough,' John Calico said. 'You've got what you wanted, Tod. Leave it be.'

The rancher feared that Tod would push too far, even for a man who was so considerate of his wife's pleading.

'*Mister* Calico,' Tod ranted. 'And say it out loud, Beck.'

Saul Beck ate more humble pie, the taste of which was as sour as gall in his mouth.

'Mister Calico,' he sang out.

'That's better.' Tod Calico's laughter was contemptuous.

John Calico knew that it had taken a mountain of courage for Beck to back down, much more than it would have taken to face up to Tod. Concern and love for his wife had been the reason, not fear. But the rancher reckoned that there might also be another reason for Saul Beck's back-tracking from trouble. Had he drawn on and beaten Tod, who was no slouch with a gun, Beck would have needed to be fast. There would have been witnesses to that display of guncraft. A fast draw attracted attention and raised questions. That he might not want.

'Now that this foolishness is over and done with,' the rancher said, 'me and the boys will see you folk safely through to Calico Junction, Beck.'

'Obliged,' Saul said, climbing on board the wagon.

As they rolled towards Calico Junction, John Calico sifted through his thoughts about Saul Beck and the way a six-gun sat so snuggly on his hip. Some men wore a six-gun for show, or as a working tool. Such guns were worn awkwardly and drawn slowly. But there were other men who wore a gun in a way that was special. Like as if it was attached to them at birth.

Gunfighters, for instance.

CHAPTER EIGHT

Calico Junction had all the rawness of a new town, undecided yet between growing and dying. The timber of many of its buildings still oozed sap. Its main drag had not won the battle with the resilient desert. Under the boardwalks it was a lost cause, where the weeds, many of them colourful and exotic, defied the progress of civilization, putting the town on notice that the fight was not yet won.

At the south end of the street stood the ruins of a Franciscan mission, once home to the brave men who had ventured West long before the ranchers and settlers to bring the word of God to the Indians. The charred roof beams of the crumbling mission, and the row of graves just within its walls was evidence of the monks' failure.

There were two saloons and a bawdy house, where the scantily clad whores leaned over or sat on the veranda, tempting passers-by to taste their pleasures. One of the women lewdly lifted her petticoats as Mary Beck went by, laughing uproariously at her embarrassment.

'If you want to lie with a real woman,' she called to Beck, 'come a-callin', honey!'

To his shame, fight it as he might, Saul Beck felt a surge of heat in his groin. There had been a time, not too long ago, when women like the whore on the bawdy house veranda, were his bedmates. Sometimes the orderly and proper couplings he had with Mary, though pleasurable, lacked the spit and kick of the unruly and improper couplings he had had with women whose only purpose for existing was to drive a man insane with pleasure.

To further embarrass Mary, two other whores joined in the petticoat antics.

'Heh, Rosie,' Tod Calico called to the youngest of the whores, an angel-faced girl no more than seventeen or eighteen years of age, 'keep it warm for me. I'll be by later.'

Beck thought he saw a knowing exchange of glances between John Calico and an older woman. The rancher was tempted to rebuke his son for his foul-mouthed exhortation, but found himself restrained by the fact that he, too, was a regular but secret visitor to the bawdy-house. His secret was known to only one man, and that was Tod Calico, whom he had bumped in to one night on his way to the house privy.

Being a man of strong urges and a widower, in no hurry to replace the shrew he had buried two years previously, the rancher had little alternative but to visit the bawdy-house for relief. There were some free and respectable women in Calico Junction and the town's hinterland, but they would only trade their company in the way that John Calico would like if there was a preacher in the wings. One day he would remarry, of course, but only when he was ready to have another woman under his feet. However, right now, the wounds from his marriage to a woman whom he often thought of as Satan's sister were too raw for the salt of another marriage to be applied.

Tod Calico stared at his father, openly inviting his rebuke, knowing full well that he could not deliver a reprimand. Irked as he was by his old man's earlier staying of his hand, he was of a mind to blurt out John Calico's secret to the whole town. But he was too much of a coward for that, fearing the rancher's retribution.

John Calico wished that there was more of him and less of his mother in his son. Tod was not a man with whom he would associate, were he a stranger. However, blood was blood, and Calico had stood and would stand by his son, though there were many things he had done which the rancher did not hold with.

The devil prodded Tod Calico to open defiance. He swung his horse under the veranda of the bawdy-house, stood on his saddle and vaulted on to the veranda. He grabbed the whore, swept her up in his arms and carried her inside. Rosie giggled and screeched as Tod Calico's hands freely explored her person.

Offended by the lewd display, as any decent woman would be, Mary Beck gasped.

'Hasn't Calico any control over his boy.'

'None of our business, Mary.' Saul Beck's tone was brusque. He turned in the wagon seat to address John Calico: 'I thank you Mr Calico for seeing Mary and me safely to town.'

'Glad I was on hand to help out,' he returned curtly. He galloped away, Tod Calico's lecherous yells ringing in his ears.

'He should horsewhip that boy of his before it's too late to rein him in,' was Mary Beck's sternly delivered opinion.

Saul Beck repeated: 'Like I said—'

'It's none of our business.'

'Right.'

Beck's mood was on the tetchy side. Pocketing his pride when he had backed down from Tod Calico's challenge had been, in his opinion, unwise. The rancher's son would see the episode as unfinished business needing conclusion. Beck reckoned that the best that had been achieved was a long-fingering of the trouble, but trouble there would be.

Swinging the wagon through the livery gates, Beck saw Tod Calico on the bawdy-house veranda, his business with Rosie being over with for the time being, its purpose of shaming and taunting John Calico achieved. From the cradle to his nineteenth birthday, when she died, Tod had been his ma's son exclusively. Hester Calico's dedication to rearing Tod in a molly-coddling fashion had, long before, earned her husband's disapproval, and because of the rancher's efforts to counter Hester's spoiling ways, she had withdrawn her affection and co-operation from John Calico. And though it had been a mistreated horse who had kicked Hester Calico in the head and killed her, in Tod Calico's mind, twisted by a hatred for his father which had been consistently and venomously fostered by Hester, there was no peresuading Tod but that John Calico's hand had somehow been involved in the tradgedy.

From the whorehouse veranda, Tod Calico taunted Saul Beck:

'Wouldn't hang 'round too long if I was you, Beck.' His laughter was a good impersonation of a hyena. 'Might catch lead poisoning.'

Despondently, Mary Beck said: 'This thing between Tod Calico and you isn't finished, is it, Saul.'

'Don't reckon it is, Mary,' he answered honestly.

'Oh, Saul,' she sighed, shoulders slumped. 'Is there no end to our troubles?'

It was a question to which Saul Beck did not have an answer.

CHAPTER NINE

'Don't know why Calico puts up with that boy of his.' The livery keeper spat contemptuously into a tumble of straw. 'That Tod Calico's badder inside than a rotten wound.'

Saul Beck, not thinking it wise to take sides, remained neutral and stuck to business.

'Your best oats and clean straw for my team,' he ordered.

The livery keeper answered gruffly, as close as a shaving to being argumentative:

'That's all Patrick Joseph Ryan's livery provides, mister.'

Beck smiled broadly. 'Never doubted it, friend.'

Ryan's glance took in Beck's worse-for-wear-garb. 'Costs plenty.'

'What's plenty?' Saul asked, conscious of his meagre resources.

'A dollar for feed for each nag. Same for straw and housing.'

'Four dollars a day,' Saul yelped. 'I'm not housing my horses in the stable at Bethlehem, Mr Ryan. Is there another livery round here?'

'Yeah.'

'Point it out, mister.'

Patrick Joseph Ryan pointed south. 'Someplace round Sonora.'

'That's in Mexico.'

'Kinda smart, your husband, ma'am,' he said to Mary Beck.

'Have you got weekly rates?' Beck quizzed the livery-owner.

'You be around that long?'

'As long as it takes for another wagon train to pass through, if it passes through,' Beck added despondently.

'Weekly rates, huh?' The livery owner scratched at the grey stubble on his chin. 'Mebbe.'

'Yes or no,' Saul said testily.

'A week is seven days—'

'Kinda smart, this livery-owner, ma'am,' Beck said to Mary.

The comeback on his earlier smart-alecry was not lost on Patrick Joseph Ryan. He smiled wryly.

'Seven days at four dollars a day comes to twenty-eight dollars.'

'That makes your weekly rates the same as your daily rates,' Beck observed.

'Are you sure you're not Irish, mister?' Ryan joked. ' 'Cause you sure run off at the mouth. Twenty-five dollars for the week. Can't be fairer than that.'

'Twenty,' Beck haggled.

'Twenty-two. Take it or leave it,' the livery-owner said, and then guffawed. ' 'Course, you could always try Sonora.'

Handing over twenty dollars from his slack poke, Beck consoled himself that with the monopoly Patrick Joseph Ryan enjoyed he could have held out for the full twenty-eight dollars and more.

'Is there a carpenter in town?' Beck enquired. 'I need him to put my wagon in shape.'

Ryan sized up the weather-beaten, trail-battered wagon.

'You sure it's a carpenter and not a darn magician you want?'

Saul glowered.

'Try the Broken Arrow.' The livery-owner pointed along the street to a saloon. 'Ask for John Patrick Ryan. My kid brother,' the livery-owner elaborated, in answer to Beck's raised eyebrow.

Ten minutes later, prised loose from the Broken Arrow, not by Saul's persuasion but by the saloon-owner's reminder about his bar bill, John Patrick Ryan was wobbling round Beck's wagon, his head shaking fit to come off.

'The Creator hisself couldn't put this load of firewood to rights, mister.'

'I know it's pretty shook—'

'Shook, you say. That rig's liable to fall 'part if I blow on it.'

More likely to go on fire, Saul felt like saying, but instead asked: 'Is there another carpenter in town?'

'Nope. And as soon as I can get a poke t'gether, there won't be a carpenter in this dogshit town either.'

Beck saw an opening.

'You'll never get a poke together by looking into a whiskey-bottle, Ryan.'

The carpenter's face took on a deep weariness.

'Don't you think I know that, mister.' He cast a longing glance towards the saloon.

Beck said, 'If you want that poke, you've got to start somewhere. Why not with my wagon?'

John Patrick Ryan again wobbled round the wagon.

'Likely I'd be taking your money for nothing,' he cautioned Beck.

'I'm willing to gamble on you being a better hammer-and-saw man than you give yourself credit for,' Saul said.

The carpenter sighed. 'No one's given me credit for anything in a long time,' he said. 'I'll work on your wagon, mister.' A spark of new-found pride glowed in John Patrick Ryan's faded blue eyes. 'And I'll do the best damn job that I know how!'

'That's all a man can ask,' Beck said. 'When can you start?'

Ryan struggled out of his coat as if he had twenty

arms, which right then he probably imagined he had.

'Why not now?'

Beck smiled. 'Sawing your hand off isn't going to get my wagon trailworthy, Mr Ryan.'

After a moment's drunken huffiness, the carpenter examined his shaking hands and laughed.

'Tomorrow morning,' he declared. 'First light. My workshop's at the end of the alley beside the general store.'

'I'll be there,' Beck promised.

Ryan wobbled off, not sure of how many legs he had. As he went past the Broken Arrow, he rejected all of his drinking buddies' exhortations to join them.

'Don't be so high and mighty, Ryan,' a mean-minded drunk called after the carpenter. 'You'll be back!'

Mary Beck came to stand alongside Saul. She put her arm round his waist.

'You're a good man, Saul Beck,' she said.

'We'd best try and find ourselves a cheap boarding-house,' Saul said. 'And hope that the bugs aren't too hungry.'

The livery-owner, who had been watching and listening to the exchanges between Beck and his brother, came forward. 'The best boarding-house in town is the Leprechaun's Fancy.'

'Who might the owner of the Leprechaun's

Fancy be?' Saul enquired of the livery-owner, already reckoning that he knew the answer.

Patrick Joseph Ryan confirmed this.

'A fine lady by the name of Kate Hannah Ryan.' He grinned. 'Who just happens to be my baby sister.'

'Now I tell you truly that I could have been racking my brains for the next hundred years and never think of that,' Saul said, sarcastically.

'You mosey 'long to Kate's. Tell her I sent you. She'll see you right.' He took from his vest pocket the money Beck had given him for livery dues and shoved it into Saul's coat pocket. 'There'll be no charge, Beck,' he said. ' 'Cause that was a mighty Christian thing you did, giving m' brother back his pride.'

'I can't expect you to feed my nags for nothing,' Saul argued.

'It won't be for nothing. I got me ways.' He turned to the expensively clad man riding up, every inch a gambler. 'Three dollars a day for best oats and a clean stall, mister.'

'Three dollars?' the rider questioned.

'You're welcome to try the next livery, if you want,' Ryan said.

'Where is it?'

'Prob'ly down Sonora way.'

'That's in Mexico!'

'How long do you plan on staying?' Patrick Joseph Ryan enquired of the new arrival.

'I was figuring on a week. Maybe a while longer if my luck's in.'

'Well now, if your 'rithmatic is as good as your geeeorgraphy,' the livery owner drawled, 'you'll know that if your week is five days that'll be fifteen dollars. And if your week is seven days, it'll be twenty-one dollars.'

The disgruntled gambler dismounted and handed Ryan the reins. As he walked away, the crusty Irishman coughed. 'Them dollars are paid in advance, mister.'

'In advance!'

'No exceptions,' the livery owner stated. ' 'Sides, you're a gambler. A gambler ain't a good bet for credit in my book. Lots of card-jugglers die of lead poisoning, you see.'

'If I'm dead you can sell my horse and saddle!'

Ryan shook his head. 'Did that once. This gambler honcho had used his horse and saddle as a stake to stay in a game of five-card stud, three times. Three fellas turned up looking. Got ugly. Shot each other. Good business for my brother Willie Ned Ryan.' He grinned at Saul Beck. 'The undertaker. But lousy for me. So if you're staying you're paying, mister,' he told the gambler.

The gambler hesitated. Patrick Joseph Ryan held out the reins of his horse for the gambler to take.

'There's always that livery down Sonora way, mister.'

Grudgingly, the gambler handed over payment.

'Does the Ryan family own this town?' Saul Beck enquired, when the gambler had taken his leave.

The livery-owner's smile was wide. 'Well, ev'rything that John Calico don't own, a Ryan owns.' He walked the gambler's horse into the livery. 'You tell Kate Hannah that you're friends of mine. 'Cause if you don't, that woman's sure got a larcenous streak in her. And I just don't know where she darnwell got it from.'

As Mary and Saul strolled along to the Leprechaun's Fancy boarding-house, Mary said:

'This town's got a good feel to it, Saul.'

'Yes,' he agreed. 'But before you go getting all cosy about this burg, remember what we set out to do. Farm in an out-of-the-way place, where no one will ever get to know who I am, honey.'

'Wonder if they've got a schoolteacher?' Mary Beck speculated.

CHAPTER TEN

Good as his word, John Patrick Ryan was at work on Beck's wagon at first light the next morning. Saul had worried that thirst might have overcome the zeal of conversion, and that Ryan would revert back to old ways. But when Beck visited his workshop, the carpenter was bushy-tailed and bright-eyed, and the wagon was already looking good. When Saul complimented Ryan and expressed his pleasure at the work already done, the carpenter got a glint of pride in his eyes which Beck suspected had not shone for quite a time.

Ryan said, 'No need to fret. I can understand why you might, Mr Beck. But I promise you that I'll repair your wagon to make it look like new.'

Three days later, work on the wagon completed, the carpenter proved as good as his promise.

'Why, Mr Ryan,' Mary Beck enthused, 'that wagon could go all the way to the moon and back.'

John Patrick Ryan stood back to examine his work, and the glow of pride in his eyes shone even brighter. Two other wagons and orders for doors and a staircase had come in.

'I'm sure glad I got in before the rush, Mr Ryan,' Saul said, smiling.

'And I'm sure glad that you started that rush, Mr Beck.'

'Isn't it about time that you two began calling each other by your Christian names?' Mary suggested. 'Seeing that you've been as thick as fleas on a dog's rump these last couple of days.'

'I guess it is at that, John Patrick,' Saul said.

'When are you folk moving on?' the carpenter asked.

'Well . . .' Mary began, vaguely.

'Soon as the next wagon train comes through town,' Saul said.

A shadow of disappointment flitted across Mary Beck's face.

'Seems you two might have diff'rent ideas on that?' Ryan shrewdly observed.

'Not at all,' Mary said. 'Where Saul goes, I go, Mr Ryan.'

Beck and his wife had had many conversations about what best to do. Saul was certain that adhering to their original plan was right. While Mary, though not wholly contradictive, was of the opinion that Calico Junction might be a nice town to settle in.

'It's a tad raw, yet,' she conceded. 'But I reckon that in no time at all Calico Junction will be a fine family town, Saul.'

Beck did not entirely disagree with his wife, though as a former gunfighter who had seen a lot of towns at a crossroads as Calico Junction was, go bad, he held his peace. Secretly he wished for nothing better than to put down roots in Calico Junction, because farming would not be an easy life for him or Mary. There would be long days of backbreaking toil, and the dangers of living in the wilderness with neighbours scattered far and wide would be great. Much of the West had been tamed, but that only pushed the desperadoes who were unwilling to conform further into the remaining wilderness, where the government free land was on offer to bring settlers to the region. The pickings were not good, settlers did not have much to steal. But that only made mean men meaner, with the result that many settlers fell to hardcase guns.

It was not hard work that he was shy of, it was Mary he feared for. She was a beautiful, elegant woman. However, she lacked the rawbone grit that she would need, isolated and alone from the kind of people she had been friendly with before she had been ostracized when she took up with him. So many times she had reassured Saul that she was well rid of those fair-weather friends, but she would turn away to hide what was in her eyes. At those times he regretted acting in his own self-interest when he had asked Mary Stratton to marry him. Their lives had run on separate tracks, and Saul often thought that it would have been better to leave it that way.

Strolling back to the Leprechaun's Fancy boarding-house, Mary said in a tone that was too casual to be impulsive:

'I was talking to John Calico yesterday. He was in town to get supplies. He said that it was well past the time for the town to have a school, Saul. Why, isn't that a pretty bonnet,' she said by way of diversion, as they passed the milliner's shop.

Saul did not respond to his wife's prompting. She had been seed-planting. He would be fair-minded with her, and give the planted seed a chance to grow.

'Real pretty,' he said.

They strolled on.

Passing the Broken Arrow saloon, Patrick Joseph Ryan, the livery-owner, crossed their path on his way into the watering hole.

'Buy you a beer, Beck?' he invited.

'Mary and me were—'

'Just strolling, Mr Ryan,' she interjected. 'I'm sure Saul would love a beer.' When Beck hesitated, but with his tongue licking his lips, Mary urged him: 'Go on. You'll just be under my feet when I'm window shopping.'

'In that case . . .'

Saul entered the saloon with the livery-owner. Settled at a table, Ryan said:

'I hear that brother of mine's done a fine job on your rig, Beck.'

'Better than just fine,' Saul confirmed. 'It looks like new.'

'Lots of work rolling in, too, I hear.'

'I've just come from his workshop, and there's a queue forming.'

'We haven't said much to each other these past coupla years. Not through any fault of mine or his. It was just the way of things. John Patrick spent his days and nights whiskey-chasing, and had no time for anything else.'

'Well,' Saul said, 'maybe you should mosey along to his workshop right now and put that to rights.'

The livery-owner nodded. 'You know, maybe I should at that. OK if I leave you to finish that beer 'lone?'

'That'll be just dandy.'

The livery-owner swallowed down his beer in one long gulp and left. On his way out, Tod Calico and four of his cronies were entering the saloon and considered that the livery-owner was in their way, though they left no room for him to pass, crowding the batwings as they were. One of the men roughly shoved Patrick Joseph aside. He was not a man of bulky stature, and the shove sent the livery-owner wheeling backwards across the saloon. He fell heavily against the solid mahogany bar and lay winded. His plight and distress were a keen sense of amusement to Tod Calico and his cohorts. Saul was surprised that the saloon's patrons, nearest to the livery-owner, did nothing to help him. In fact they pointedly turned away.

Beck hurried to help the livery-owner, whom he now considered a friend.

'Leave him be!' Tod Calico barked.

'He's injured,' Saul said.

The rancher's son pouted mockingly, and wiped away imaginary tears from his cheeks.

'Why, ain't that sad, boys.' And, mimicking Saul: 'He's injured.'

Beck ignored Calico's play-acting. He went to Ryan's aid. Bent over, his backside was too much of a temptation for Tod Calico to resist. He placed his boot on Beck's rump and pushed hard. Saul shot forward, and was fortunate to avoid a headlong collision with the bar, which no doubt would have done serious damage, but he could not avoid sprawling on the saloon floor.

Tod Calico sniggered. 'Wonder if he's injured too, fellas?'

When Tod Calico's eyes swept the bar, the amusement at Beck dragging himself off the floor went through the saloon like a bushfire fanned by a gale. Beck's fists balled.

'Leave it be, Saul,' Patrick Joseph said.

Calico, his hand hovering over his six-gun, sneered.

'That would be real wise, Beck.'

Saul was not of a mind to be wise or co-operative. But again the livery-owner urged restraint.

'Best if you help your friend over to Doc Wright's office 'cross the street,' Tod Calico advised Beck. 'I think he's busted his shoulder.'

Beck helped Ryan to his feet, his face a mask of pain. As they left the saloon, Calico and his hard-case pals began chicken-clucking. The laughter from the saloon reached all the way across Main to Wright's office, where Saul slammed the door hard to shut it out.

Edward Wright, a Bostonian who had come West to practise what he called real medicine, as opposed to pandering to the foibles and hypochondria of wealthy Bostonians, had often regretted his impetuously zealous decision, and had by way of consolation taken to drinking copious amounts of rye. Luckily, on this day, he had once again sworn off alcohol after the demons of a week-long bender.

'Tod Calico?' the medico asked Beck.

'Yep.'

'Saw him ride in. When Tod Calico rides in, trouble isn't ever far behind.'

While he was tending to the livery owner's shoulder, which he had confirmed as close to broken but not quite, Saul asked:

'If Tod Calico's trouble, why do you folk put up with him, Doc?'

Wright snorted. 'Easy to see that you're as new in town as a nickel leaving the mint.'

'That doesn't answer my question,' Saul Beck persisted.

Wright finished strapping the livery-owner's shoulder, with the advice:

'You rest up for a couple of weeks, Patrick Joseph. And no lifting or hauling, you hear?'

'I've got a business to run, Doc,' the livery owner growled.

'Well, you had better get use to the idea that, for a spell, that business is going to have to more or less run itself.'

'Damn! A thousand damns!' Ryan swore. 'Maybe I should have let you whip that bastard Tod Calico, Beck. Might have too, if there wasn't five of them and one of you.'

Saul grinned. 'You seem mighty sure that I could have, as you say, whipped Tod Calico.'

Ryan sized up Saul Beck. 'I figure that if you slipped that leash on you, you could handle Tod Calico and his cronies.'

Beck scoffed. 'Leash?'

'Yeah,' the livery owner repeated. 'Leash.' Ryan's gaze settled on Saul Beck. 'Your stance over in the saloon was, I reckon, the stance of a man who's no novice in dealing with curs the likes of Tod Calico and his pals.'

Beck took up a lazy, casual stance.

'Sure it isn't his skull is busted up instead of his shoulder, Doc?' he said humorously.

The livery-owner did not comment further, but Beck could see the wheels inside his head turning, as the wheels inside John Calico's head had been turning on their journey to town after the Indian attack. Altogether too many wheels turning for his liking. The sooner a wagon train passed through town, the better he'd like it. Until then he'd have to play a hand that gave no further hint of his past. Obviously, he had already shown too many of his cards for comfort.

'And,' Wright warned Ryan, 'you can't tend to yourself either. You mosey along to the Leprechaun's Fancy and let Kate Hannah nurse you.'

Ryan, laughed. 'No can do, Doc.'

'Why not?'

His grin was wide. 'Can't afford her charges. 'Sides, I can't sleep without the smell of hay and hosses. Like some men can't sleep without the scent of a woman.'

'I can sleep fine without both,' Wright declared, his glance going to the open desk drawer to a bottle of whiskey. The medico's Adam's apple bobbed with an oncoming thirst. 'Now get out of here,' he growled, his pledge to become teetotal vanishing faster than snow in hellfire.

Once outside, Ryan said, 'I sure hope that no child needs delivering, or no one is unlucky 'nuff to get gunshot in the next coupla days.'

Tod Calico was lounging on the Broken Arrow porch swigging from a whiskey-bottle, flushed, and in an ugly mood. With hooded eyes he watched Saul Beck, his mood becoming more ugly by the second. The fact that the stranger had had the gall to show defiance to him was eating through him like a rampant cancer. Tod Calico was used to men kowtowing to him, and their fear was a drug to which he had become addicted. He worried that Beck's show of defiance would tempt others to emulate his example. If enough got the courage to do so, his days as Calico Junction's top dog would be in jeopardy. Being a man of shallow character, his standing mattered a whole lot to Tod Calico. Saul Beck was a threat to that standing. And he was not of a mind to let the stranger change the town's pecking order.

'Damn you, Pa,' he muttered. 'Why the hell didn't you leave him to the Apaches!'

Beck saw the sulking rancher's son out of the corner of his eye, and knew that no matter how hard he tried to avoid it, trouble in the name of Tod Calico was coming his way.

CHAPTER ELEVEN

Kate Hannah Ryan placed a meal fit for a king in front of Saul and Mary Beck and told them that they could stay, free of charge, for as long as it took.

'Won't cost you folks a cent.'

'I thank you kindly, Kate Hannah,' Saul Beck said. 'But Mary and I would prefer to pay our way for as long as we can.'

'That's so, Kate Hannah,' Mary agreed.

The boarding-house proprietor shooed their objection to her hospitality aside.

'If you want to stay, you stay free of charge. Or else you're damn well out on your ear!' She addressed Saul: 'I don't know how you did it, Mr Beck. But you've given my brother John Patrick back his self-respect, and Patrick Joseph tells me that you were ready to square up to Tod Calico today in the Broken Arrow when that cur struck him down. That, in my book, makes you the kind of man that this town sorely needs, before it becomes a haven for Tod Calico and his nest of vipers. Vipers attract vipers. Soon this town will be overrun with trash!

'Now eat up. That there is bacon and cabbage from an Irish recipe that will still have your mouth watering for more if you live to be a hundred. Then,' she told Mary Beck, 'you'd best get an early night. Those kids will be quite a handful, having never had no learning afore now.'

'Kids?' Mary asked, wide-eyed.

'You're a teacher, ain't ya?'

'Yes.' Mary was puzzled. 'But how did you know that?'

'Was dusting your room. Knocked over that trunk of yours. It sprang open. Saw those teacher's books. Wasn't prying, mind. Tomorrow morning you'll have twenty odd brats waiting for you in the church hall. We ain't got no school yet, 'cause we never had no teacher to teach in it. But if you want to be that teacher, I'll knock heads together at the next town meeting coming up in a week or so to make that happen. Though I reckon it won't pay much.'

Saul Beck could see a light in his wife's eye that he had not seen glow for a long time. If there was one thing above anything else that she missed since marrying him, Beck knew that it was teaching. Mary was an excellent teacher, but more important than that, she liked children and took pride in turning them into fine adults.

'It's learning will finally end the day of the gun in the West,' Mary had told Saul, shortly after making his acquaintance. 'And that can't be a bad thing.'

'Thank you, Kate Hannah,' Mary said, tears welling up in her sea-blue eyes. 'It'll be good to be in a classroom again.' She glanced quickly at Saul, with pleading in her gaze. 'But of course it will only be until we can join a wagon train, you understand, Kate Hannah.'

'Wagon train!' the owner of the Leprechaun's Fancy yelped. 'Why not put down roots here in Calico Junction. In Tod Calico you saw it's bad side. But there are good people here too.' Her eyes fixed on Saul. 'Looking for someone to lead them. You could be that man, Saul Beck. This town needs good folk like you.' Kate Hannah studied Beck. 'My feeling is that you ain't always been lily-white pure, mister. But if you had bad ways, then I reckon that they're behind you. Maybe you should bury the past right here in Calico Junction.'

Beck's answer was a brusque one. 'Like Mary said, Kate Hannah, we'll be moving on as soon as a wagon train comes through.'

Just then another guest arrived, looking for a room. Saul was relieved that Kate Hannah had not had the chance to pin him down with a whole pile of questions as to why he was so eager to move on. Though they had plotted their story well and had rehearsed it a thousand times, the more questions asked, the more pitfalls opened up.

'That will be fine, ma'am,' the new guest said, agreeing without quibble to Kate Hannah Ryan's outrageous terms.

Saul Beck tensed. He immediately shifted his chair to show his back to the hall where the new guest was, and to hide Mary from view.

'What's got into you, Saul Beck,' Mary said, as she misinterpreted his leaning towards her.

'I'll see you to your room, Mr Thomas,' Kate Hannah said.

'That's Colonel Thomas, ma'am. Colonel Rufe Thomas, at your service.'

Mary Beck now understood her husband's antics. The colour washed out of her face.

Going upstairs, Thomas explained to Kate Hannah:

'I'm here to visit an old friend, John Calico. He was a captain who served with me in the war. A fine officer. I want this to be a surprise visit, so I'll be obliged if you'll not say a word, ma'am.'

'You can count on me,' Kate Hannah assured Thomas.

Now Beck knew where he had seen John Calico before. In one of the many photographs on Rufe Thomas's dining-room wall.

'I'll want to be hiring a rig tomorrow to drive out to the Circle C ranch,' Thomas told Kate Hannah.

'Leave it to me,' she said. 'I'm a good friend of

the livery-owner. A man known for his reasonable rates.'

Though Beck's troubles were mounting, Kate's description of her brother's business strategy brought a wry grin to his face.

'It's been almost two years, Saul,' Mary said. 'Maybe Thomas won't—'

'Sure he'll remember,' Saul interjected. 'Men like Rufe Thomas never forget anything.'

'What are we going to do?' Mary fretted.

'Not much we can do. If he heads straight out to the Calico ranch, maybe the wagon train will show before he gets back to town.'

'Yes. Of course,' Mary said, clutching at straws in a gale.

'Or we can leave town. Wait outside until Thomas leaves. When he's gone, we can come back into town.'

Mary pointed out the obvious flaw in this plan.

'If we do that, Saul, a single wagon setting out with Apaches on the warpath will stir a heap of curiosity about the loco pair on board.'

Mary Beck's point of view was a valid one. Saul Beck felt a noose tightening round him, and it was getting tighter by the second.

CHAPTER TWELVE

John Calico's sleep was disturbed by his son's rowdy return from town. Disgruntled, joints aching, he got out of bed and went downstairs to confront Tod. Half-way down the stairs, observing his son's disgraceful condition, he rebuked him:

'You dishonour my house, boy!'

Tod had slid down the wall, unable to get back up, so deep was his drunken stupor. The rancher spotted the man who had delivered Tod home sneak out the front door.

'Hold up!' he commanded.

The man ignored the rancher's order. John Calico hurried downstairs and grabbed his six-gun from his gunbelt on the hallstand. He yanked open the door and cut loose at the two shadows hot-footing across the moonlit yard. One of the men screamed and clutched at his upper arm.

'Hold up like I said,' Calico ordered the wounded man's partner, who was still running. 'Or you'll not be so lucky.'

The man halted.

'Turn round,' the rancher barked. On recognizing the man, Calico said, 'I might have known that it would be you, Harrington. Clear out now. You too, Long,' he ordered his whining partner.

'Clear out, huh?' Harrington growled, his drunken mood ugly.

'Ride or die!' John Calico said, his tone heavy with menace. To ram home his point, the rancher's bullet bit at Bud Harrington's right toecap. He leapt about in a drunken dance, as if the soles of his feet were on fire. 'Clear out now. Both of you.'

Tod Calico staggered to the door.

'They're my buddies, Pa.'

'They're vermin – trash,' the rancher barked. 'Best rid of.'

'If they're my friends, does that make me trash too, Pa?' Tod Calico argued rebelliously.

John Calico looked his son steadily in the eye and answered: 'If you choose them over me and my kind, then that makes you trash too, Tod.'

Seething, Tod Calico raised his hand to strike his father.

'What are you waiting for, boy?' the rancher challenged him, offering his face to Tod. 'You've done everything else.'

John Calico turned to go back inside, but not before he warned Harrington and Long:

'Come morning, if you two are still here, I'll kill you.'

'You fellas wait in town, you hear?' Tod called, as

the duo lost no time in mounting up.

When Tod turned back into the house, his father told him:

'You sleep in the barn. And I mean the barn, not the bunkhouse. There are hard working, decent-living men in the bunkhouse. Don't disturb their sleep.'

'In that case I just might return to town, Pa.'

'If that's your choice.'

Tod Calico's grin was evil. 'Maybe I'll even sample Maisie Owen.'

The modicum of respect and love that John Calico had left in his heart for Tod dried up at that moment. Maisie Owen was the only woman in Calico Junction's bawdy-house with whom the rancher shared a bed. He had his desires, but he was not a wanton philanderer who hopped from bed to bed. Maisie Owen was the oldest of the women in the bawdy-house, and at forty two was long past the younger bucks' attentions. In fact she was exclusive to the rancher on his twice weekly visits. To everyone else she was just another whore. However, Calico had got to know the woman as well as the whore, and had found Maisie Owen to be part of the herd but not of the herd.

Maisie was a widow woman who had unwisely married a man who loved liquor and five-card stud more than her, and had paid the price at the gambling-table for being caught dealing from a deck with too many aces.

Of late, John Calico was thinking more and more about asking Maisie to be his wife and the mistress of the Circle C. His courage was not yet strong enough to pitch folks' opinions to blazes, and he worried, too, that Tod would give Maisie a hard time. But he would get round to asking, of that he was certain.

Maisie Owen was a good woman, treated badly by cruel fate.

'See who the better man is, Pa,' the drunken Tod Calico taunted his father.

When he spoke, the rancher's voice was a mere croak, so constricted by anger were his vocal chords.

'Get out of my sight, Tod,' he said. 'Before I kill you, so help me God.'

Tod Calico sobered on seeing the devil rear up inside his father. He backed out of the house. On reaching the porch he took off on a gangling run, checking behind him all the way to the barn.

Debilitated by his coal-hot anger, John Calico sat on the stairs and wept.

Later, his fear in check, Tod Calico crept out of the corner of the barn he had been crouching in, his old brashness restored. He saddled a fresh horse. At half after midnight, the night was still young and town would be full of pleasures to taste. But he would not go through with his intention to demand the services of Maisie Owen, because she was simply not worth dying for, and that's the price he would surely pay if he was foolish enough to push his old man more than he already had.

On reaching town, he sought out the company of Bud Harrington and his sidekick Francey Long, the men whom John Calico had put legs under. They were not hard to find. As usual they were bellied up to the bar in the Broken Arrow, telling anyone who bought them a beer about the events at the Circle C. Long's shirt was stained with the dried blood from his shoulder wound, which was just a nick. The nostril-clogging scent of the blood and month-old sweat meant that beers were slid their way rather than personally presented.

Spotting Tod Calico coming through the batwings, Long nudged Harrington.

'Why, hello there, Tod.'

Bud Harrington's greeting was full of boisterous *bonhomie.*

Francey Long, who secretly hated Tod Calico, but saw the sense in currying favour to avoid a lot of the back-breaking work at the Circle C, sniggered.

'You booted off Calico property, too, Tod?'

Tod Calico's features froze. 'No one kicks me off anywhere!' he snapped.

Long was quick to concur. 'I know that, Tod. Can't you take a joke?'

Calico slapped Long on the back. 'Sure I can, Francey. But most times, I prefer them to be at someone else's expense.'

The men who had been hanging on Harrington's and Long's words drifted away from their company, not wanting to earn Tod Calico's displeasure, since the gist of their conversation up to his arrival had been none too complimentary to any man bearing the name of Calico.

'Set 'em up, Larry,' Tod told the barkeep, and announced: 'The drinks are on me!'

The long bar was suddenly full of jostling men, grabbing the beers which Larry filled and gulping them back to get a refill before Tod Calico's largess ran out of steam, because everyone knew that his impulses to be generous were infrequent and short-lived.

Drinking together at a table in a dim corner, Bud Harrington, feeling a sudden urge for female company, suggested to Tod Calico that they visit the bawdy house. Francey Long was quick and eager to endorse Harrington's boredom-relieving suggestion. Both men were taken aback when the rancher's son rejected the idea, because they knew him to be a man of gargantuan appetites.

'Then what're we goin' to do, Tod?' Francey Long whined.

Tod Calico's grey eyes danced with a hellish malice.

'You know, it's a kind of cold night, ain't it?'

'Huh?' Harrington grunted, bemused.

'In fact a night for a nice fire,' Tod said.

'Fire?' Long was puzzled.

Tod Calico looped his arms round his partners'

shoulders and joined their heads to his.

'Fellas,' he said. 'I've got me an idea for some real fun.'

CHAPTER THIRTEEN

The first hint of trouble for Saul and Mary Beck was when their sleep was interrupted by the sound of the town fire-bell. Saul got quickly out of bed, his senses already telling him that the furore on the street would have dire consequences for them. He went to the window and looked out. Then, before hurrying from the room, Beck cautioned his wife:

'Stay here.'

'What is it, Saul?'

'If my knowledge of the town's geography is right, it looks like the carpenter's workshop is on fire.'

'The wagon, Saul,' Mary fretted.

'All we can hope for is that Ryan left it outside the shop.'

'Without that wagon . . .'

'Hush,' Saul said, kissing Mary on the forehead. 'No use worrying until we know the worst.'

Outside, Saul joined the men scampering down

the alley that led to the carpenter's workshop, filling buckets from the horse-troughs as they passed. A bucket was thrust into Saul's hand, and he joined in the useless effort to quench what was by now an inferno.

'Ryan's shop is done for,' the leader of the fire-fighters shouted. 'But the sparks will ignite other buildings. So let's concentrate on keeping them from catching fire.'

Saul Beck, his hopes fading, ran round to the back of the blazing building and found that his despair was justified. There was no sign of his wagon, which could only mean that Ryan had housed the wagon inside the now burning building, which left him and Mary stranded in Calico Junction for the foreseeable future, until he got the money together to buy another wagon or have one built.

And right now there was no chance of his being able to do that. Of course Mary would have a wage, but it would likely be barely enough to pay their way, if that.

Saul rejoined the fire-fighters to prevent the flames and sparks claiming the general store which, being directly across the alley, was the structure closest to the carpenter's workshop. And if that building caught fire, there was a whole row adjoining it which it would be impossible to save with buckets of water. That would mean that one side of Main would end up as charred rubble.

For the next hour, men laboured frantically to dampen down the flying sparks and scorched debris of the workshop, reduced now to a smouldering ruin. With the fire contained and the excitement abating, it was Kate Hannah Ryan who asked:

'Did anyone see John Patrick? I checked. He's not at home.'

Men looked at each other for the answer, but the general response was one of shaking heads. Then eyes turned to the heap of debris which had been the carpenter's workshop. Slowly at first, fearing to have their worst fears confirmed, Saul and the other men toe-poked the fringes of the ill-fated ruin, but gradually their search became more frantic until, under a charred roof-beam, they found the carpenter's blackened remains. Men turned aside, gagging at the stench of the carpenter's scorched flesh.

The common perception was that John Patrick Ryan had slipped back into old ways.

'Prob'ly knocked over a lamp,' one man opined.

It was an opinion which Saul Beck hotly contested, and not just out of misplaced loyalty to a man whom he had begun to call his friend. Beck simply did not believe that John Patrick Ryan would have let go of his new-found respect and self-esteem.

'The last I saw of John Patrick,' another man said, 'he was puttin' the finishin' touches to your wagon, Beck.' The information did not help Saul Beck's conscience any. 'He surely took a whole passel of pride in resurrectin' that ramshackle rig of yours.'

'Liquor is a demon that most men find almost impossible to master, once it's got hold of a fella,' a smoke-blackened firefighter said. 'I saw John Patrick earlier tonight goin' past the saloon with the kind of haunted look a man gets when a thirst builds in him. I'd say he was tossing up right then and there about goin' inside.'

'John Patrick did not go on a bender!' Saul Beck glared at those speculating so. 'Any of you men see him in either of the saloons tonight, or at any time since he swore off the grog?' Beck quizzed.

No one had.

'Well, then,' Saul Beck said, 'I figure that what I say is true. John Patrick was sober when his work-shop caught fire.'

'If that's so, Saul,' Kate Hannah Ryan asked, logically. 'Why didn't he just run out of there while he had the chance?'

Beck said sombrely, 'A man can only run if he can put legs under him, Kate Hannah.'

'What're ya sayin', mister?' the leader of the fire-fighters asked.

Saul knelt beside the carpenter's remains to examine the bump on his head behind his right ear.

'It's just a bump,' the leader of the fire-fighters

said. 'That ain't so darn strange when this whole place caved in on him.'

'It would be a pretty accurately aimed, or very unfortunate missile to have caused a bump just behind his ear,' was Beck's response. 'It isn't an easy place to hit.'

'I guess,' the man agreed, thoughtfully taking on board Beck's reasoning.

'What're you saying, Saul?' Kate Hannah enquired.

Beck thought for a long time, carefully considering the shape of the bump on the carpenter's skull, before answering. When he did give his opinion, it brought a gasp from the assembled crowd.

'I figure that this bump on John Patrick's skull was made by the butt of a six-gun. And that John Patrick did not high-tail it when the fire started, because he was out cold. Likely dead.'

'But that would mean that . . .'

Kate Hannah Ryan struggled with the enormity of Saul Beck's conclusion.

'That your brother was murdered, Kate Hannah,' Beck flatly stated.

CHAPTER FOURTEEN

About a mile outside of town, each inch of the trail back to the Circle C sending daggers of pain into his chest, Tod Calico ordered his cohorts to draw rein.

'We gotta keep goin', Tod,' Bud Harrington urged.

'Yeah, Tod,' Francey Long added. 'We've barely been movin' since we left town.'

'Damn you!' the rancher's son yelled. 'I think Ryan's busted me up good with that plank of wood he swung at me.' Calico held his left side. 'Wouldn't surprise me any if he busted a coupla ribs.'

Harrington and Long, out of favour at the Circle C, were of a mind to high-tail it for the Mex border as fast as their nags would take them.

'I never planned on no murder, Tod,' Harrington griped.

'Yeah,' Long, equally sour, whined. 'Murderin' Ryan was in no plan, Tod.'

'Was I suppose to let him floor me with that plank of wood?' Tod Calico argued.

'Torchin' and murder are diff'rent,' Bud Harrington flung back. 'Now we're facin' a rope, if'n we're caught, Tod.'

'You did the killin', Tod,' Francey Long said.

Seeing the drift of his partners' thinking, the rancher's son warned:

'If one of us is guilty of murder, then we all are. That means that we've got to stick together. Besides, if I say that it was one of you who killed Ryan, who do you think will be believed?'

'Sure, Tod,' Long placated Calico. 'We're in this t'gether. Ain't that so, Bud?'

However, when again Tod dropped behind, fighting to remain in the saddle, Long's opinion was: 'I sure as shit don't want no rope round my neck, Bud.'

'Me neither,' Harrington said, and then slyly added: 'But we don't have to hit the trail to Mexico penniless, Francey . . .'

'Yeah, reckon not,' Long agreed. 'What've you got in mind, Bud?'

'That bulgin' safe in old man Calico's office.'

'Must be thousands of dollars in there.' Long dreamed.

'There is,' Harrington confirmed. 'I know for sure.'

'How?' Long wanted to know.

'A coupla months 'go I was in the house with Tod. The time that John Calico made that trip back East. Tod went to the safe to get the cash to pay for a coupla hundred longhorns that were delivered to the ranch . . .'

'I remember,' Long said.

'I can tell you that my eyes popped when I saw them stacks of bills. So if we're booted off the Circle C, and facin' a rope if any one cottons on to the fact that that dent on Ryan's skull was made by the butt of a six-gun, I figure that what's in that safe is our due, Francey.'

'I reckon so too, Bud.'

Riding close together they planned their treachery, but had not anticipated that with each hoof fall the journey to the Circle C would become slower and more arduous, until now it had stopped dead in its tracks as Tod Calico swayed in his saddle, eyes rolling.

Harrington and Long conspired again.

'At the rate we're travellin',' Harrington said. 'It'll be light before we reach the ranch. And that means that there'll be plenty o' men 'round the place for the old man to call on, when we heist that safe.'

'What 'bout Tod?' Francey Long said, glancing back at the slouched figure of the rancher's son.

Harrington grinned wolfishly. 'I reckon that 'nother sore spot won't make much diff'rence,

Francey.' He fell back alongside Tod Calico. 'How're you doin', Tod?' he enquired with false concern.

'Not so good, Bud,' the rancher's son said muzzily.

'Don't you worry none,' Harrington falsely reassured Tod. 'Francey and me will see you safely back to the ranch.'

He fell back a couple of feet behind Calico and slipped his .45 from its holster. He swiped the barrel of the gun across the back of Tod's head. The rancher's son toppled headlong from his saddle. He crashed heavily to the ground and lay still.

Harrington sniggered. 'What goes round comes round, Tod.'

Long said, concerned, 'I think you've killed him, Bud.'

'Makes no diff'rence whether I did or not!' Harrington growled, not taking kindly to his partner's criticism.

Long's worry deepened.

'Wounded, John Calico might in time forget. But if Tod's done for, he'll hunt us down like rabid dogs, Bud.'

'He's got to find us first, ain't he. And south o' the border is a big place for him to go lookin'.'

'Mexico ain't big 'nuff,' Long opined. 'Calico's got a long reach, Bud.'

'We'll go to Honduras then. Mebbe Peru.'

'All of South America won't be big 'nuff if Tod's dead,' Francey Long gloomily predicted.

Irked, Harrington snarled: 'Ain't nothin' we can do 'bout it now!' He swung his horse around. 'Let's go get that loot in Calico's safe.'

'Without a wagon, what are we going to do?' Mary Beck wanted to know of her husband.

It was a question to which Saul Beck had no answer. They could hide from Rufe Thomas until he left town to visit with John Calico, but they could not hide for ever. Thomas would be visiting town during his stay at the Circle C. They could bump in to him at any street corner. Beck cursed his luck, that of all places to find himself in, it had to be a town where Rufe Thomas had an old army buddy to visit with. He had taken great care to cover his tracks and his past, but it had all been for nought. The luck he had had as a gunfighter had deserted him as an honest man. He could only think that the devil's luck of his former profession had, on his turning his back on Satan, become the devil's curse.

Again, Saul Beck had his regrets about asking Mary Stratton to marry him. His life was developing along the familiar lines of a man with his past – always on the move when trouble reared its head again.

If the folk of Calico Junction learned of his past, he would not be welcome among them. Gunfighters were the lepers of the West. When people wanted the services of a gunfighter to clean up their messes, he was only welcome for as long as it took to get the job done. Because any town giving refuge to a gunfighter invited trouble.

Beck was pondering on his predicament when Patrick Joseph Ryan, the livery-owner, called on him.

'Saul,' he said, 'you figure that my brother was murdered, don't you?'

'I do.'

'Any ideas on who the killer might be?'

Beck shook his head.

'Like to find out?'

'I'm no Pinkerton,' Saul said. 'I'm a—'

'What?' the livery-owner bluntly interjected. 'You sure as hell ain't no settler.' He took hold of Saul Beck's callous-free hands. 'Not with these, you ain't.' He then looked to Mary Beck. 'And if you don't mind me saying so, ma'am, you're no settler's woman either. You talk too good. And you look too good.'

The silence following on Ryan's shrewd assessment dragged to a full minute before he spoke again:

'Gunfighter, I'd say. But I don't really mind, Beck. In my book a man's past don't matter much. To me, right now, you're a good man. That's all that matters.'

Saul and Mary Beck exchanged glances and reached a silent agreement.

'Gunfighter,' Beck confirmed.

Patrick Joseph Ryan shook his head. 'Figured so. I have a proposition. Tod Calico killed my brother, of that I'm certain. I'll pay top dollar. You can haul him back to town to hang. Or you can kill him where you find him. Don't matter much to me.'

Mary Beck looped her arm through Saul's, and drew him close to her side.

'Such money would be a killer's bounty, Mr Ryan. Saul and I want no part of it.'

'Ma'am,' the livery-owner said, 'we ain't got any law here that I can turn to. The last two sheriffs were run out of town by Tod Calico and his cronies. Now no one wants the job, and I can't say that I blame them. Because any man pinning on a star in this town will sooner or later have to deal with Tod Calico and his clique.'

He considered the Becks.

'Now, let's be sensible here. You folk need money and a new wagon.' He addressed his next remarks directly to Saul Beck. 'I'll give you one thousand dollars and a spanking new wagon in return for Tod Calico's neck in a noose, or a bullet in his black heart. My proposition will solve all your problems, folks.'

Saul Beck, though sorely tempted, backed his wife's stance.

'My days for collecting a killer's bounty are over and done with, Patrick Joseph.'

A glow of pride shone in Mary Beck's eyes.

Ryan shook his head soberly. 'In that case,' he said, 'you're going to have to work hard and long to get a wagon under you, Beck.' He massaged his injured shoulder. 'It'll mean a fourteen-hour day forking hay, watering and feeding nags. But the livery job is yours, 'til this shoulder of mine works proper again. The only help you'll have is a half-wit boy. His name is Hal, but most times he don't know that. Sometimes, too, he forgets to wake up. If he does wake, he starts work at sun-up. Sleep you'll have to get when you can.'

Tears gushed from Mary Beck's eyes.

Beck said, 'I thank you, Patrick Joseph. You'll get your fourteen hours a day, every second of which I'll work as hard as I know how.'

'Don't doubt it,' Ryan said. 'You ready to start work now?'

'This minute.'

'Then let's go. I've got nags lined up for feeding, and stalls to be cleaned out.'

Saul grabbed his hat and joined Ryan. Strolling to the livery, Beck asked:

'What're you going to do about your brother's killer?'

'Simple. Hire me a gun. Or do the job m'self.'

'That I wouldn't recommend trying. Too dangerous. Tod Calico's a natural killer. You wouldn't stand a chance, Patrick Joseph.'

The livery-owner stopped mid-stride, his face grim.

'For the last coupla years, Tod Calico and his hardcase pals have ruled this town through fear. If he's not stopped, it can only get worse. The fact is, that every man jack in this burg buried their heads in the sand, hoping that John Calico would rein in his boy. He didn't. Guess he can't. Now,' Ryan said with gritty determination, 'it's time to cut Tod Calico down to size.'

Beck said, 'Don't you need evidence against Tod Calico, Patrick Joseph?'

'No other man hereabouts fits the bill as neatly as Tod Calico. There was bad blood 'tween John Patrick and Tod Calico, going back a spell, since John Patrick slapped him down for insulting Kate Hannah. Since John Patrick kicked his thirst for liquor, Tod Calico's been saying that John Patrick was getting too uppity. Needed to be taught a lesson. I figure that's what Calico did last night.' He studied Beck. 'And you're a damn fool if you think that Tod Calico will ignore you for long more, mister. You're a challenge to Calico. He'll know that if he leaves you sucking air, one of two things will happen. You'll become top dog in the pound. Or you'll chase all the dogs, including him, right out of the pound. Either way it'll be over for Tod Calico. He'll not let that happen without a fight to the end.'

'I'll be moving on,' Saul said. 'Tod Calico knows that.'

'Moving on, huh? Then you'll be stepping over

Tod Calico's body on your way out,' Ryan predicted.

The livery-owner strolled on. He had not told Saul Beck anything that he did not already know. All he could hope for was that he could hold off a confrontation with Tod Calico, and be gone before he worked up the nerve to force his hand.

But he doubted it.

CHAPTER FIFTEEN

John Calico was a man whose day started at first light. Though he was probably the territory's richest man, he was not one to sleep in. Riches he did not see as an excuse for sloth. Today he was up before first light. His night had been a restless one, thinking about a son who was bound for hell if he did not change his ways. Calico was a name that he had made synonomous with fairness and rightness, and Tod's antics were staining that reputation and the name of Calico.

Like any father, he wanted to be proud of and protect his son. However, Tod had sullied his name, and had stretched his ambition to care for him to breaking point. Tod was weak – easily swayed. He had surrounded himself with pandering trash. John Calico knew that up to now, Tod and his hardcase friends had had it easy, and that success at browbeating folk had given Tod a sense of reputation far in excess of his ability. Now things in Calico Junction had changed.

The rancher's thoughts turned to Saul Beck. Right off there had been bad blood between him and Tod. Some men just rubbed each other up the wrong way, and it became inevitable that sooner or later bad blood led to gunplay. What troubled John Calico was that in pushing Beck, Tod might just bite off more than he could chew. Saul Beck was a man of swiftly moving eye, hand and thought. His gait and demeanour were not those of a natural homesteader. He had a gut-feeling about Beck. The rancher reckoned he recognized the species. He was fearful that Tod would not. And if he did, recognition might make Saul Beck an even greater challenge. Probably Tod's final challenge.

Maybe he could talk to Beck. Arrive at some kind of understanding.

John Calico's reverie was interrupted by the sound of breaking glass. At first he thought that it was Tod wandering home drunk. But then he got a cold feeling along his spine; the kind of feeling that had warned him of trouble brewing in the days when he was carving out the Circle C under threat from Indians and a bevy of desperadoes, who'd rather plunder another man's hard work than consider honest labour themselves to become his equal.

Calico took the six-gun he had used the night before from the bedside bureau drawer. He went and eased open the door of the room, hoping that its upper fickle hinge, despite frequent oiling, would not alert the intruders, because he was now certain that that was what he had to contend with. Blessedly, the contrary hinge remained silent. Stepping into the hall, John Calico immediately sought the cover of a deep shadow at the top of the stairs.

'What if he wakes up?'

The rancher instantly recognized Francey Long's whining voice.

'If we're fast,' came Bud Harrington's raspy tone, 'he won't. Not 'til we have a gun to his head. And you know, Francey, I've been thinkin' over what you said 'bout old man Calico huntin' us down if that whack I gave Tod on the skull puts him to sleep for good . . .'

Shock almost made Calico react too soon. A shot in the inky darkness might or might not find a target. But it would certainly send Harrington and Long scurrying for cover, and he would have lost the element of surprise needed to deal with a couple of snakes.

'. . . Well,' Harrigton continued, 'once he opens that safe, we won't need the old coot any more.'

'And what if Tod ain't dead,' Long worried. 'He'll come lookin' too.'

'There ain't no problem there,' Harrington reassured his *compadre* in mayhem. 'Before we hit the trail for Mexico, we'll slip a note under Patrick Joseph Ryan's door. He'll take a shotgun and blast Tod into hell, for sure.'

'Heck, Bud. You're a real slick thinker,' Long complimented.

John Calico edged deeper into the shadows as Harrington and Long started upstairs. It looked like Tod had finally chewed off more trouble than he could swallow.

But first things first . . . .

So excited and pleased had Saul Beck been at finding work, he had not given any thought to how a job as livery-man could mean trouble. The danger flashed before him when he saw Colonel Rufe Thomas leave the Leprechaun's Fancy boarding-house and turn towards the livery. Of course he would want to hire a horse or rig to journey to the Circle C.

It was well past sun-up. Beck cursed that of all mornings, Hal, the livery boy, had chosen to sleep out. On came Thomas. There was no way out of his predicament that Saul could see.

The game was up!

CHAPTER SIXTEEN

'Best if you find a shadow, Saul.'

Beck swung round on the livery-owner's advice.

'I'm guessing that by the way you're skulking that that gent means trouble for you.'

Beck had no time to explain before Rufe Thomas hailed Patrick Joseph Ryan.

'Keeper, I'm looking to hire the best rig you've got.'

Climbing the ladder to the loft, Beck was seething that once more he was backtracking, an activity that was beginning to stick in his craw.

'Then, sir,' Ryan hailed back, matching the colonel's commanding voice, 'you've come to the right man and the right place.' He glanced back to check that Saul was out of sight. 'If you step this way, you'll leave this establishment in such a veeheeicle.'

'I'm on my way to pay a surprise visit on my friend John Calico,' Thomas informed the keeper. 'Calico and I used to be fellow-officers. A fine officer and gentleman.'

'John Calico's a fine upstanding gent, sure enough,' Ryan agreed, but added bitterly: 'But that boy of his is a lowdown, sidewinding, black-hearted, no-good son-of-a-bitch skunk!'

Rufe Thomas was shaken.

'That's fighting talk, if I ever heard it,' he said.

'You tell him that Patrick Joseph Ryan said so. And if he wants to do anything 'bout it, I'll be right here waiting. You still want that rig?'

'Is there another livery round here?'

'Sure is.'

'Point it out if you would, sir.'

Ryan pointed.

'I don't see any other livery,' Thomas said.

'That's 'cause you can't see all the way to Sonora.' Ryan chuckled.

'In that case I don't have a choice, do I?' Thomas growled.

'No. You damn well don't!'

Ten minutes later, as the livery-owner saw off Thomas, Saul Beck joined him in a critical mood.

'That was a damn fool thing to do,' he rebuked Ryan. 'When Thomas conveys your message, Tod Calico will come riding in looking for your hide. And if he doesn't, then John Calico will.'

'What then?' Beck angrily questioned Ryan, worried that the man who had shown him kindness would end up wormbait.

'We'll have to wait and see, won't we,' was Ryan's carefree reply.

Just then a sleepy-eyed Hal strolled along to the livery.

'Do you know how much darn trouble you've caused, boy?' Saul chastized the hapless livery-hand.

Peplexed, Hal scratched his tousled mop of russet hair.

'Trouble, mister? I ain't even been here.'

'That,' Saul said, beady-eyed, 'was the trouble.'

John Calico hoped that the fast rising sun shining through the landing window would not penetrate the shadow he was hiding in for another ten seconds or so. Bud Harrington and Francey Long were half-way up the stairs and within easy shooting range, but Calico wanted to wait until he was eye to eye with the treacherous duo before he blasted one and hoped to get the information about Tod from the other, before he dispatched him.

Harrington looked through the staircase banister to Calico's closed bedroom door.

'It's awful quiet, Bud,' Long worried. 'Calico's an old man, and old men snore,' he reasoned.

Bud Harrington's response was an impatient one.

'Not all o' them.'

'Most all that I know,' Francey Long argued. 'Mebbe he's 'wake, Bud? Waitin'.'

Harrington scoffed. But Long had planted a

seed whose roots gnawed their way through his confidence, and brought a sheen of perspiration to his brow. He said grimly:

'Well, we ain't backin' out now!' He dragged his lagging partner alongside him. 'We're in this together, Francey. You got other ideas?'

Long gulped. 'No, Bud. I ain't got no other ideas. Honest I ain't,' he added, cowering under Bud Harrington's searching glare.

They came up the stairs, the sun slanting at an angle that would soon reveal Calico. The seconds which Harrington and Long had wasted arguing were precious seconds that might yet work against the rancher. Best to act now, he reckoned. John Calico stepped out of the shadows, six-gun cocked.

'Holy sh—'

Bud Harrington never got to finish his oath. Calico's .45 spat. Harrington was blasted off his feet, a gaping, ragged hole in his belly. The force of the bullet pitched him over the banister and down into the hall. The house reverberated with the six-gun's explosion. The rancher's gun swung to cover a transfixed Francey Long.

'What did you rotten bastards do to Tod?' Calico demanded. His second demand was: 'And what's this guff about Tod being a murderer?'

Long, a cunning man, saw a light at the end of a dark tunnel. Now that Harrington was dead meat, the rancher needed information he could trade to maybe weasel himself out of his predicament.

Calico might still shoot him once he had the information he needed. But he would definitely shoot him if he held out. Francey Long was not a gambling man. But he was gambling now.

'If I tell ya where Tod is, I walk free,' he bargained.

The rancher fumed: 'You're in no position to make demands, Long. Talk or I'll drop you where you stand.'

Long sneered. 'A dead man can't talk, Calico. And right now Tod ain't in such a good condition. Needs tending to. Fast.'

The rancher knew that he was in a bind. It galled him to have to meet Francey Long's terms, but if he gave his word he'd keep it.

'Talk and walk,' he agreed.

Relief flooded through Long. He had no fears about the old man going back on his word. Men of John Calico's calibre did not do that. He was a tough-as-nails *hombre*, but a bargain struck was a bargain delivered.

Long began his narrative of events.

'Last night, Tod had this idea for some fun and games. We burned down John Patrick Ryan's workshop. On'y when we busted in to torch the place, Ryan was sleepin' in his shop. Me and Harrington wanted to call it quits, but when that saw-and-hammer man took a swipe at Tod with a plank of wood, Tod busted his skull.'

Intense anguish crimped Calico's features. He

staggered back against the staircase wall.

'That makes Tod a murderer, Calico,' Long gloated. 'And it ain't like no killin' he did afore. Ryan never had no chance. Tod'll hang for this. Unless,' Long's voice took on a sly note, 'there ain't no witness to tell what happened.' Francey Long sighed. 'Always did fancy livin' in the South Americas. On'y with empty pockets . . .' He shrugged.

John Calico's rage roared through him. Long cringed, held up his hands and backed down the stairs.

'I just got total loss o' mem'ry, Mr Calico,' he whined.

'Where's Tod?' the rancher asked in a voice strangled by fury.

'He's over in Brody Pass. Bud whacked him good. None o' my doin'.'

'Get out of my sight before I forget my bargain, Long,' Calico barked.

Francey Long's leaps took him downstairs to the hall in double-quick time. He was racing along the hall when the front door burst open and two ranch hands, alerted by the shooting and quickest to reach the house, blocked his path. Seeing their boss holding on to the stairs, close to collapse, and Bud Harrington's bloodied remains in the hall, they asked no questions of Long. Both men's guns exploded. Long was driven back along the hall to lie dead beside his partner in skulduggery.

*

Saul Beck watched proudly as Mary walked to the church hall where children were filing in for their first class. Folk congratulated, thanked and praised Mary. The years which had piled on her since she had become Mrs Beck had vanished, and Beck was seeing Mary Stratton, the cocky, confident woman who had ridden the stage with him to Pennington.

Patrick Joseph Ryan summed it up:

'That woman of yours has been reborn, Saul. It's going to be hard to uproot and leave now.' The livery-owner observed his new employee. 'Maybe there's no need to go on from here. Maybe this town won't be as critical as you think, Saul.'

Saul Beck's smile was a sombre one.

'That's a whole stack of maybes, friend,' he said drily.

Ryan sighed contentedly. 'You know, Saul. I've got me a feeling right in here,' he rubbed his belly, 'that good times are a-coming for Calico Junction.'

'Maybe they are at that,' Beck said. 'But they won't come without trouble.'

The livery-owner sagely observed: 'Nothing worth having ever comes without trouble, Saul. The only question is, is it worth fighting for?'

John Calico, his face tight and pale with worry, leaped from the rig he was driving on seeing Tod Calico lying still and pale.

'Is he dead, boss?' Abe Cronkite, Calico's foreman enquired, upon the rancher's examination of his son.

'If he isn't,' the rancher said, 'he's as good as. We've got to get him back to the house fast.'

Cronkite was the only man Calico had brought with him to search for Tod; the only man he could explicitly trust in the fifty or so whom he employed. Abe Cronkite was the first man he had hired, and he had never once regretted his decision. Through the years, hard and troubled to begin with, Abe Cronkite had been much more than just a hired hand. He had been a friend and confidant.

Five years previously, in appreciation of Cronkite's steadfast loyalty, John Calico had cut out a hundred acres, had a house built on it, and had given his foreman fifty longhorns. He had reduced his hours on the Circle C, too, to enable Cronkite to work the small spread. His progress during that time had been steady.

'Sure hope that you won't be trying to buy me out one day, Abe,' Calico had recently joked.

Cronkite wrapped Tod in the blankets the rancher had brought with him, and placed him gingerly on the rig. Tod moaned.

'Thank God he's still alive,' Cronkite said.

The foreman observed the dried blood on Tod Calico's shirt where the carpenter's blow had done its damage. He then glanced at the soft, sandy soil where Tod had fallen, and saw nothing that could have inflicted the injury hinted at by the blood-staining. He turned enquiring eyes John Calico's way.

'There's nothing I can hide from you, is there, Abe?'

The rancher shared the awful burden which Francey Long's narration had placed on his shoulders. Abe Cronkite wished that, on this occasion, the rancher had not confided in him. Being privy to the details of a cold-blooded murder did not settle easy with him. Killing to protect a man's kith and kin was one thing, but murder as attributed to Tod Calico was something entirely different.

Observing Abe Cronkite's unease, Calico sought his foreman's assurance that the secret he had shared with him would remain between them.

'I have to have your promise that you won't blabber, Abe. No matter how uneasy your conscience becomes.'

'You've got my word, Mr Calico,' he reassured the rancher. And prayed that keeping such a secret would not rot his heart and, in the end, present his soul to Satan.

They were drawing near to the Circle C when Rufe Thomas cut their path.

'Howdy, John,' the colonel hailed the rancher. 'Thought I'd pay a surprise visit.' Calico was stunned. Thomas's curious gaze went to Tod Calico. 'What happened to Tod, John?'

'Thrown by his horse'

In the absence of a response from Calico, who was still coming to terms with Thomas's surprise appearance, Abe Cronkite had told the lie.

'Looks pretty bad,' was Rufe Thomas's observation.

'You can help, mister.' Again Cronkite had taken the initiative. 'Ride back to town and get Doc Wright out to the ranch house, pronto.' He climbed out of his saddle. 'Use my nag. It'll be faster than a rig.'

When Thomas was mounted on Cronkite's horse, John Calico spoke for the first time to urge all haste.

'Ride like the wind, Rufe,' he pleaded.

'Be back before you know I'm gone,' Thomas reassured the rancher.

Saul Beck went about his work with an easy gait and an even easier mind. Rufe Thomas would be John Calico's guest by now and out of the way for a spell, which would give him and Mary time to think over their next move. He heard the thunder of hoofs arriving in town. He was curious, but not troubled.

CHAPTER SEVENTEEN

Saul Beck was forced to leap aside as Rufe Thomas flashed past on his way to Doc Wright's office, which was situated on the street below the livery. He thought that he had caught a glance of interest in him from Thomas, but Saul was hoping that his shabby working garb combined with the colonel's haste would prevent recognition. He immediately sought the inner reaches of the livery, leaving the tidying-up chore he was occupied with until later.

Despite Beck's order to stay put, Hal had run after Thomas to join the curious queue outside the doc's office. He was back within minutes with the news about Tod Calico.

'Seems he's awful busted up, Mr Beck,' Hal said, with the kind of glee that bad news is often delivered with. 'He might even die, Mr Calico's friend says.'

'Haven't you got chores to do, boy,' Beck reprimanded the youngster, as he was again about to take off for the doc's office.

'Aw, gosh, Mr Beck,' Hal moaned.

'Get to them,' Saul ordered the boy. 'You'll not earn your pay hanging around outside the doc's office.'

Dejected and sulking, Hal set about the tasks that needed tending. Then he brightened up.

'I guess we'll get all the news an'way when Mr Calico's friend comes to the livery for a fresh horse. His is all tuckered out.'

'Well, you see that he gets the best nag we have then,' Saul said. 'I've got some chores to do around town.'

'Whatcha goin' out the back way for, Mr Beck?' Hal enquired, puzzled.

'Because I darn well feel like it!' Saul barked.

Beck hated the skulking life he was being forced to live. It was not fitting for a man to have to slip and slide around the place to do his business. However, he was not his own master any more. He had to think of Mary, and her peace of mind. But he wondered for how long he could keep hiding, and pocketing his pride. Much more of the same and Mary would find herself married to a bootlicking man. Because Saul Beck figured that the more a man ran away, the more of his pride and self-esteem he lost every time he turned away from trouble. If he was not careful, skulking would become a way of life. He looked round the town backlots where a half-dozen drunks were sleeping off the revelry of the night before, and swore then and there that come what may, he had his tail between his legs for the last time.

'Boy!'

Beck stiffened as he heard Rufe Thomas's shout through a crack in the rear wall of the livery.

'Yes, sir,' Hal replied in awe.

'Go get the keeper. Tell him I need a fresh horse.'

'Mr Beck ain't here, sir . . .' Saul tensed. 'But I can saddle up the stallion over there for ya. He's faster than the wind and stronger than Samson.'

'Yes. You do that, boy.' There was a pause. 'Beck, you say, is the keeper's name?'

'Yes, sir,' Hal confirmed.

'Own this place for long?'

'Mr Beck ain't the owner, sir. That'd be Mr Ryan. Mr Beck just works for Mr Ryan. Started only this very mornin'.'

'You don't say. And he's gone missing already, huh?'

'He had some chores to do in town. Just left in the last coupla minutes.'

'Chores in town, huh? Left in the last couple of minutes, you say? I didn't see anyone leave, son.'

'Mr Beck went out the back way,' Hal informed Thomas.

'That a fact. Shy kind, huh? Mighty odd indeed,' Thomas concluded. 'Beck been in town long?'

'No, sir. A coupla days. Came in with a busted-up wagon.'

Saul Beck could almost hear the wheels turning in Colonel Rufe Thomas's head. He probably had the answer already. But if he had not, it would not take long for him to find it. He heard the jingle of coins as Thomas paid for the stallion.

'I'll have one of Calico's hands deliver it back, boy.'

'Yes, sir.'

Another jingle of coins. 'For you,' Thomas said.

'Gee, mister,' Hal said in awe. 'Two whole dollars.'

'Now, tell me, boy. Where does this fella Beck live?'

'Not sure,' Hal said vaguely. 'But I reckon, maybe the Leprechaun's Fancy.'

'That's the best and most expensive boarding-house in town, son. A man needs lots of money to board there. Has this Beck *hombre* got that kind of money? Doesn't seem like it to me, if he's shovelling horse manure for a living.'

Hal said, 'Him and Mr Ryan are kinda pally. And Mr Ryan's sister Kate Hannah owns the Leprechaun's Fancy. So I reckon Mr Ryan might've done a deal with his sister for Mr Beck.'

Rufe Thomas chuckled. 'You haven't got as big a hole in the head as folk might think, son.'

Hal giggled. 'Whatcha talkin' 'bout, mister. I ain't got no hole in m' head.'

Beck heard the clop of hoofs. He hurried round to the side of the livery to observe Thomas. As he rode along Main, the colonel's pace was leisurely, his eyes scanning the boardwalks and stores.

Once Thomas had cleared town, Saul Beck made fast tracks to the church hall, the location of the temporary school. As he approached an open window to get Mary's attention, he could hear the children laughing. He took up a position at the side of the window and peered through. Mary was sitting in the centre of the floor, the children in a circle around her. One blond little boy with the most expressive blue eyes was doing an impression of some unknown adult.

Mary chided him. 'Now, Arthur, that's quite enough. You've got to have respect for your elders.'

However, a gentle smile was on Mary Beck's lips. She was the happiest Saul had seen her in a long time. He pulled away from the window and walked slowly back to the livery. He had started out with the idea that they would use the last of their meagre resources to take the stage, due in town in a couple of hours, serving Calico Junction once every two weeks. But on the evidence he had just seen, to leave now he would surely be stealing away his wife's happiness.

Hal's greeting was: 'Heh, Mr Beck. That gent who burned up the trail into town a while back was in here, and he was mighty interested in you.

Asked a whole pile o' questions. Friend of yours, Mr Beck?'

'Kind of,' Saul said, and took a broom to sweep the stalls with.

Beck was certain that by the time Rufe Thomas reached the Circle C, he would have him pegged. And if he told John Calico who he was, Tod Calico would see him as an even greater challenge than he already was. That was, of course, if Tod Calico survived whatever life-threatening injury he had received.

But whether Tod Calico survived or not, Saul knew that he had a long-term problem if he remained in Calico Junction. When he had changed his mind about taking on the assignment which Thomas had paid his passage to Pennington for, the colonel's furious response was to promise that one day he would even the score with him.

Whatever way matters panned out, of one thing Saul Beck was now certain. Before much longer he would be buckling on a six-gun again. Or he would be running once more.

'Damn,' he murmured, furiously sweeping the stall he was in, 'I've done all the running that I'm going to do. I'm not running one more inch!'

CHAPTER EIGHTEEN

It was the second day of Tod Calico's coma. Doc Wright had taken up residency in the Calico house to constantly monitor Tod's every moan and quiver of his eyelids. There was not much he could do, other than offer John Calico the assurance of his presence. He had been totally honest with the rancher.

'There's little I can do, John,' he'd told him. 'Tod will either come out of it or . . .' He changed the drift of the conversation. 'That injury he's got on his side. I don't reckon that he got that falling from his horse, John. Has all the signs of some kind of blow. Do you know anything about that?'

'Pa . . .'

The weak summons from Tod Calico's bedroom saved the rancher from having to give an answer to the medico's question. Both men rushed into the room to find Tod half-raised in the bed, bleary-eyed and foolish.

'Tod, you're awake.' The rancher rushed to his

son's side. 'Thank the Almighty!'

Doc Wright helped Tod back on to his pillows with the advice:

'Take it easy, Tod. Rest a spell. See how you feel.'

'Feel?' Tod laughed weakly. 'My head's the size of this darn room.'

Wright held up his finger. 'Try and follow my finger, Tod.'

He moved his finger back and forth across Tod Calico's eyes.

'Well?' John Calico asked anxiously.

'Who am I, Tod?' the doc asked.

Tod giggled childishly. 'Who are you? Don't you know who you are, Doc?'

'I think he's going to be fine, John,' Wright told the rancher.

Tod Calico lay back on his pillows, but only for seconds before he shot up again, fighting both the doc's and his father's restraint.

'I'm going to kill that Bud Harrington and Francey Long,' he snarled.

'They're already dead, Tod,' Calico said.

'Dead?'

'Dead,' John Calico confirmed.

'Shit!' the rancher's son cursed. 'I wanted to peel their damn skin off inch by inch.'

When he was settled back down, Wright asked, 'That wound on your side, Tod—'

'Thank you for staying on, Doc,' John Calico interjected. 'But now that Tod's all right, I'm sure that you've got other patients to tend to back in town.'

The sawbones was a touch peeved at his abrupt dismissal, but he was not about to buck Calico. The rancher was a good man, but it was well known that getting on his wrong side could lead to all sorts of problems for a body.

'You be sure to give me a call if Tod—'

'Sure will, Edward.'

The friendly use of his Christian name took the sting out of the rancher's starchy dismissal. Wright figured that John Calico already knew the cause of his son's injury. He reckoned that he did also. And if he was right in his thinking that Tod Calico and the fire at John Patrick Ryan's carpentry workshop were linked, then it would be best that he treat the injury and forget his questions.

'I'll drop by tomorrow. But I guess lots of rest is the best medicine for Tod right now, John.'

'I'll see that he gets all the rest he needs, Edward.'

Rufe Thomas, who had been left to his own company during the crisis, came from the study as the rancher closed the front door on Wright's departure.

'Good news, John?'

'The best, Rufe. Sorry I haven't been around for the last couple of days after you coming all the way from Pennington to visit.'

'Oh, I understand, John. Couldn't be helped.'

As John Calico went past on his way back upstairs, Thomas said:

'Did you know that you've got a gunfighter in town?'

'A gunfighter?' Calico asked worriedly, instantly aware of the kind of challenge a gunfighter would be to Tod once he was back on his feet.

'An *hombre* by the name of Saul Beck.'

'Beck, huh?' the rancher grunted, his thoughts on Beck now making sense. 'Figures.' Calico explained the sequence of events that had brought Saul Beck to Calico Junction. 'Should have left him to rot out in the desert!' the rancher concluded bitterly. He studied Thomas.

'How do you know Beck, Rufe?'

'Hired him out once. Had me some trouble with nesters. Paid his passage to Pennington, but when he showed up he was already a reformed man after sharing a stage journey with Pennington's new schoolteacher. Turned my offer down flat. Didn't please me any. Told him that one day I'd even the score with him.

'Maybe that day's come.'

CHAPTER NINETEEN

Mary Beck looked on, fretting as her husband took his gunbelt from the wooden chest into which he had put the Colt .45 the day he had married her.

'Don't look at me so, Mary,' he said. 'What choice do I have?'

'You promised me on our wedding day, Saul, that you'd never again buckle on that belt.' Beck averted his eyes from Mary's hurt gaze. 'Sooner or later this was going to happen, wasn't it,' Mary said bitterly. 'I guess you felt pretty naked without a six-gun on your hip.'

'That's not so,' he flung back. 'And I wouldn't be putting iron on now if I could avoid doing so. But I figure that Tod Calico won't be able to resist the chance to build a reputation, and killing Saul Beck will put him well on the road to being the desperado which in his heart he wants to be.'

He gripped Mary's arms, and held her when she tried to break free of his hold.

'And even if Tod Calico gets sense and decides

not to risk throwing his life away, there's always Rufe Thomas to consider. I figure that he's a man who holds a grudge and a promise to settle accounts in equal importance. He'll hire trouble or cause trouble himself.'

Caught between the good sense of Saul's reasoning, and her fear for the danger that packing a gun would bring, Mary pleaded: 'Maybe if you rode out to the Circle C and talked to Tod Calico – Rufe Thomas, too . . .'

Seeing the fear in his wife's eyes, Saul Beck felt his resolve slip. Was it possible that Calico and Thomas would listen to any words of pacification or reason he might utter? Or would their reaction be that he was grovelling? Which would mean that he would have lost their respect, and in the process have made himself a target of ridicule and disrespect. If that was the outcome of any discusion with Tod Calico and Rufe Thomas, then he would be in an even worse position than he already was.

Mary continued with her plea: 'Talking might work, Saul. Try it for my sake, if not your own. And for Luther.' She massaged her swollen belly. 'Or Kate.'

Beck smiled. 'That's cheating, Mary.'

'A woman has to use a little blackmail every now and then when her charms fail, husband.'

He held her fiercely for a long while, and wished that he would never again have to let her go. He had fallen hopelessly in love with Mary Stratton on the stage trip to Pennington, and every second since that love had deepened.

'Luther?' he asked.

'If it's a boy.'

'Kate?'

'Well, I've been thinking that it just might be a girl, Saul.'

'Don't I get to have any say?' he gently chided her. 'I was thinking maybe of Saul, if it's a boy.'

'Don't like the name.'

'Huh?'

'Sorry. But,' she kissed him on the cheek, 'the way I see it is, that a cover doesn't make the book, so a name doesn't make the man.' She pointed to her chest. 'The good man comes from in here in his heart, Saul. The kind of man who can change his ways and do what's right and proper. Like you have.'

Saul put his arms round his wife's waist and lifted her high above him, and then let her slide down the length of his body so close that a quirly paper would not have fitted between them. After he had kissed her long and passionately, he said:

'I'll talk to Tod Calico and Rufe Thomas, Mary.'

'Thanks, Saul,' she said quietly. 'I'm looking forward to long and lazy sunsets on the porch with you when our time is counting down.'

Saul Beck put his gunbelt back into the wooden chest. He prayed that it would gather dust and rust over the years ahead, and hoped that time was not already, as Mary had put it, counting down.

Tod Calico woke from a long sleep to find Rufe Thomas standing by his bed. He grinned.

'Howdy, Colonel Thomas.'

'You're looking well, Tod,' Thomas said.

'Feeling good, too.'

'Mighty glad to hear it.'

John Calico came into the room. His eyes flashed angrily at Thomas.

'I said no visitors, Rufe.'

Thomas flourished the *Calico Junction Gazette*, the town's news-sheet.

'Thought Tod might want to get acquainted with what's happening in town, John.'

The rancher scowled, not believing a word of Thomas's explanation. He had served with him during the war and gave him credit for being a good officer and shrewd tactician. But he also knew him to be a devious man who would use anyone or any situation to further his own interests.

'There's a whole pile of interesting news in town right now.'

Tod Calico sat upright, his interest razor-sharp keen, the ghost of fear haunting his eyes.

'What kind of news would that be, Colonel Thomas?' he enquired tentatively.

'Rest, Tod,' John Calico said, his eyes burning holes in Rufe Thomas.

'Yes, son,' the colonel said. 'You listen to your pa's good advice.' He strolled to the doorway. 'Seems some fella called Saul Beck has a real interesting theory about the town carpenter's mur . . . I mean death, of course. Did you know that this fella Beck's a gunfighter?'

Thomas slid out of the room, his seeds of apprehension and goading sown. Tod would fret about the carpenter's murder coming to light, which, in a town with no law of its own, would bring a US marshal visiting. He'd also see Saul Beck as an even bigger challenge. Fear and pride would be the devil's tools.

John Calico had two worries. One was that his son would be revealed as John Patrick Ryan's murderer, and hang. Or, if he escaped that fate, Tod's inevitable settling of accounts with Saul Beck.

Going downstairs, pleased as a kitten after mother's milk, Thomas murmured: 'Well, now. Who'd have ever thought that my trip to see my old pal John Calico would have turned out to be so goddang interesting.'

Leaving the house to take a breath of air, Thomas saw a rider approaching across the pasture to the south of the ranch house, from the direction of town. To the colonel he was, at first, just another rider, until his attention was got by the man's ramrod-straight bearing in the saddle. Thomas had had long experience of seeing men of the approaching man's demeanour, and it had always spelt trouble. Of one thing Thomas was certain, the rider was not on a social visit. And he shrewdly guessed that the business the man had come on might very well be in relation to Tod Calico's part in the town carpenter's demise.

He was aware that since his performance in Tod Calico's bedroom, he was not in John Calico's good books. So he figured that the visit of the dourly approaching rider might just give him the chance to redeem himself in the rancher's eyes. With that in mind he popped back inside to collect a rifle, and then made his way to the barn. He climbed the ladder to the loft. The yard was deserted. All the hands were gone about their various chores. The rider had chosen his time well.

Rufe Thomas prised loose a couple of slats in the wall of the loft, and then bellied down on the floor. He got the rider in his sights, and tracked him every inch of the way up to the ranch house, where he held him steady in the Winchester's sights.

The grim-faced man dismounted, shotgun in hand.

'Tod Calico,' he called out. 'Show yourself!'

Rufe Thomas depressed the Winchester's trigger to within a hairsbreath of firing. He saw a second rider coming out of the trees to the north of the house, and whereas the man in the yard had

146

an air of determination, the new rider had the slouch of a man more on a mission of hope than one of certainty.

My, oh my. This day is just chock-full of interesting developments, Thomas said to himself.

John Calico stepped from the house.

'I don't appreciate callers toting shotguns, Ryan,' he rebuked the livery-owner.

'Don't care much what you like or dislike, Calico,' Ryan grunted. 'I've come to take Tod back to town to stand trial for the murder of my brother as soon as a US marshal and a judge gets here. I've sent for both.'

'Tod had nothing to do with John Patrick's death. He wasn't even in town that night. He was right here in the house playing cards with me and Abe Cronkite,' the rancher said, despising his lie. But it was lie or risk Tod's neck to a rope.

John Calico, expecting Ryan's visit, but not a shotgun-toting one, had schooled Cronkite in what to say if he was asked. And though reluctant to become embroiled in a murder cover-up, Cronkite had agreed. John Calico had treated him decently, and he figured that lying to save the rancher's son from a hangman's rope would pay his account in full.

'Liar!' Patrick Joseph Ryan spat. 'Abe Cronkite would go into hell and bring back the devil's tail if you asked him to. His word ain't worth spit!'

The livery-owner shouted up at the house.

'Tod Calico. Stop skulking. Come face me.'

'Tod isn't well right now,' the rancher said.

Ryan growled, 'My brother John Patrick is dead, Calico. And your son killed him.' He levelled the shotgun on the rancher. 'Now, he comes out, or I'm going in to get him.'

From the window of his bedroom, Tod Calico watched the confrontation in the yard. Normally he was full of bravado, but these weren't normal times. The bootlickers, of which Bud Harrington and Francey Long had been the most ardent, weren't around to back any play he might choose to make. And he did not care one jot for facing an enraged man toting a Greener. Shotguns made mighty big holes.

'Calico!' Ryan roared. 'I'm coming to get you!'

The enraged livery-owner walked towards the house. Rufe Thomas steadied his aim.

'Don't be a fool, Ryan,' John Calico pleaded. 'You kill Tod, and so help me before this day is out you'll join him.'

Ryan said, 'That's a price I'm willing to meet to see your son pay for murder, Calico.'

The rise of ground on which Saul Beck emerged from the trees gave him a bird's-eye view of the stand-off in the Calico yard. He instantly recognized his employer and feared for his well-being. He also would not want any harm to come to John Calico, due to his kindness in coming to his rescue

148

in the desert, and the hospitality he had shown him and Mary.

Being a man who loved and respected horses, Beck was loath to dig his spurs into the mare he was riding, but saw no option but to reach the Calico yard as fast as he could. However, he knew that irrespective of how good a head of steam he got up, there was no way that he was going to reach the yard before gunplay broke out. Patrick Joseph Ryan was marching towards the house, and John Calico was taking up a stance of stoppage.

Then Saul saw the glint from the barn loft, bright as a diamond. The livery-owner had his back to the barn and had obviously not seen it. Because if he had he would have recognized the deadly danger in that flash of sunlight on, Beck reckoned, the barrel of a rifle. There was a shooter in the barn loft. And it could only be seconds now before Ryan was cut down in cold blood.

Six-gun blazing and hoofs thundering, Beck galloped towards the ranch.

Rufe Thomas held his shot. There was more trouble on the way. And as Saul Beck got closer, the colonel's smile was a wide and smug one. He changed the angle of his rifle to cover Beck. It was time to settle accounts.

The former gunfighter would never make it to the ranch yard.

CHAPTER TWENTY

Thinking that it was one of Calico's men charging to Tod Calico's rescue, Patrick Joseph Ryan spun round, shotgun ready to cut loose. Aware of the danger, Beck shouted: 'It's me, Patrick Joseph. Saul Beck. Behind you in the barn loft,' he warned the livery-owner.

Ryan's reaction to Beck's warning, though swift, was not fast enough. He sprinted for cover behind a water trough, but cried out as Rufe Thomas's bullet smashed his leg. He staggered backwards on one peg, before crumpling to the ground. Before Thomas could get off another shot, Saul Beck was out of the saddle, his rifle blazing at the barn loft. He dragged Ryan to the side of the ranch house out of Rufe Thomas's line of fire. From the side of the house he cut loose with a double volley, before running in a zigzag pattern across the yard. Just as he dived through the barn door, a bullet from Thomas's Winchester smashed

151

the heel of his boot, and sent a shock wave up his leg that made it temporarily useless. His left leg buckled under him; he stumbled headlong and crashed into a support beam. The side of his head struck the beam and sent him reeling. His rifle flew from his grasp. The barn swam before his eyes. With his eyesight scattered he was a sitting target. Thomas, not one to miss an opportunity presented to him, casually lined Beck up for killing.

'That's enough, Rufe!'

John Calico filled the barn door.

'I've got a score to settle with Beck, John,' the colonel said.

'Then you'll have to settle it in another time and another place,' the rancher stated unequivocally.

Thomas said, 'Let me finish this, John. Now that Tod knows who Beck is, he won't rest until he faces him, you know that.'

'Beck will be long gone before Tod is on his feet again,' the rancher said. And addressing Beck he said, 'There'll be a stage through here tomorrow, Beck. I'll give you five thousand dollars to be on it when it leaves.' The rancher took Saul Beck's hesitation in responding as a ploy to twist his arm for more. 'Ten thousand.'

'You're loco, John,' Rufe Thomas declared. 'Why hand over ten thousand when a bullet will conclude this business.'

'What do you say, Mr Beck?' Calico asked.

By now Saul's senses were back with him. 'Yours is a mighty generous offer, Mr Calico. But if Mary wants to remain in town, all the money you've got won't get me to leave. Because she hasn't been as happy in a long while. I won't take that away from her.' He offered: 'I'll talk to Tod to try and make him see the insanity of going up against me. Maybe he'll listen.'

'John,' Rufe Thomas scoffed, 'Tod won't stand a chance, if he doesn't listen. You could be throwing away Tod's life right now if you don't let me finish what I started.' The turmoil of the rancher's thoughts were clearly to be seen on his face. 'Tod's well-being should be your only concern. Let me kill Beck.'

'There's been too much killing,' the rancher barked. After long consideration, he said, 'If your wife accepts my offer, Beck, will you take it?'

Beck nodded. 'I'll do what Mary wants, Mr Calico.'

The rancher relaxed. 'Then so be it. You talk to your wife. Come visit tonight and let me know your decision.'

'John . . .'

'That's an end of it, Rufe,' the rancher rebuked Thomas, then sighed: 'At least for now. But,' he told Beck, 'I'll have you know that when push comes to shove, I'll do whatever it takes to save my son.'

'I wouldn't expect anything else, Mr Calico. If

Mary is agreeable to leave, all we'll need is a wagon and supplies. Nothing more.'

'You'd turn down ten thousand dollars?' Calico asked in disbelief.

'Yes,' Saul said. 'You saved Mary's and my life out in the desert. That's payment well above any fistful of dollars.'

John Calico said sincerely, 'I pray that this matter can be settled, Mr Beck.'

'Me, too,' Saul replied.

'Aren't you forgetting something, John,' Rufe Thomas said. 'Even with Beck out of the way, Tod will still have to stand trial for that carpenter's murder.'

Calico said, 'To prove murder there has to be solid evidence.' He turned to face Beck. 'And I don't know of any.'

Beck answered honestly: 'It is my belief that Tod killed John Patrick Ryan. But evidence? I haven't got any, other than my own conviction.'

'Then,' the rancher said, 'I guess I'll have to wait until I reach the pearly gates to find out what my Maker thinks about my turning a blind eye to the acts of my son. And if He decides that there's a price to pay, then so be it. Go talk to your wife, Mr Beck.'

Saul was about to leave when a shot rang out. He and the rancher rushed from the barn together. Patrick Joseph Ryan was crawling across the yard, trailing blood in the dry dust from the gaping wound in his back. Tod Calico was pacing the dying livery owner.

'I fixed the bastard good, Pa,' he gloated, and landed a boot in the dying man's side.

'Leave him be, Tod!' the shocked rancher ordered his son. 'Help me get Ryan inside the house,' he requested of Saul Beck. 'Then I'll be obliged if you'll ride to town to get Doc Wright out here.'

'No trash like Ryan is going in the house, Pa,' Tod barked.

He levelled his six-gun on the stricken livery owner. John Calico paled to the pallor of death.

'I said leave Ryan be, Tod.'

Tod Calico sneered, and cocked the Colt .45.

'One in the head should—'

John Calico grabbed Saul Beck's six-gun to back up his order.

'Drop the gun, Tod.'

Tod Calico, once he got over his surprise, sneered.

'You won't use that, Pa. I'm your boy.'

'Don't make me, Tod,' the rancher pleaded.

After a couple of tense seconds, the rancher's relief was palpable when Tod holstered his gun.

'OK, Pa. I'll do what you want,' he said amiably.

But Saul Beck was not fooled by Tod Calico's smile. Because his eyes had the chill of a born killer.

'Duck,' he shouted at John Calico. But he was

too late. Tod's gun was already flashing back out of its holster. Beck shoved the rancher aside as Tod's gun bucked. John Calico, too mesmerized to feel the pain, looked at the blood seeping through his shirt where the bullet had grazed him. In shock he dropped the six-gun he had grabbed from Beck.

Saul dived for the gun. A bullet spat dirt in his face as his hand clutched the .45. He rolled over, triggering the gun twice. Both bullets hit Tod Calico in the chest. His own reflex action, as he grabbed his chest, put another bullet from his own gun in his gut.

'Pa,' he cried out in terror.

The rancher caught Tod in his arms as he toppled forward, dead.

'No need to go anywhere now, Beck,' he said, quietly weeping.

Rufe Thomas, immobilized by the surprising turn of events, soon got over his shock. He drew a bead on Saul Beck, ready to backshoot him. A loose board in the barn loft knocked him off balance just as he triggered the Winchester, and his bullet only grazed Beck's shoulder.

Anger as hot as hell's coals coursed through Beck. He pivoted about just in time to see Rufe Thomas line up another shot. His six-gun flashed. Thomas screamed, and toppled head first from the barn. When his anger cooled, disgusted, Saul Beck threw his gun away from him.

*

The weeks passed into months. Months into years. Time healed. Calico Junction had many new buildings and more under construction every day, as new settlers were made welcome. A new school had been built to accomodate the influx of new students. Two new teachers had been recruited to work under the guidance of its principal, Mary Beck. The town had a new infirmary, a second medico and a nurse. It also had a second general store, needed to supply the goods for the expanding community. The name over the door was: BECK'S EMPORIUM. John Calico was a fifty per cent owner. Luther Beck would soon be able to help his father in the store after school.

Saul Beck had almost learned not to watch every new rider arriving in town. One day a man might come looking. So be it. He would live for the happiness of today, and let tomorrow bring what it may. He marked the price on a new batch of brooms, and was happy doing so. He would be closing the store early today. He had the duty of best man to perform at John Calico's marriage to Maisie Owen.